KING ARTHUR
AND HIS KNIGHTS

Retold by
Felicity Brooks and Anna Claybourne

Illustrated by Rodney Matthews

Designed by Kathy Ward and Linda Penny

Edited by Anna Claybourne

Series Editor: Felicity Brooks

Series Designer: Amanda Barlow

First published in 1998 by Usborne Publishing Ltd, 83-85 Saffron Hill, London EC1N 8RT.
First published in America 1999.

Printed in Spain.

CONTENTS

The Sword in the Stone   4

Excalibur   13

The Gathering of the Knights   22

The Cursed Sword   31

The Tale of Sir Launfal   44

Sir Gawain and the Green Knight   55

Sir Tristram's Tale   67

The Enchanted Ship   78

The Scheming Sorceress   87

Sir Orfeo   93

Sir Gawain and Lady Ragnell   104

The Adventures of Sir Lancelot   114

The Search for Sir Lancelot   122

Sir Lovelyhands   132

Lancelot and Guinevere   142

The Last Battle   149

Who's who in the stories   156

Who was Arthur?   160

CHAPTER ONE

THE SWORD IN THE STONE

"**P**lease can I come with you?" begged Arthur. "Please?"

He was watching his father and brother as they saddled their horses. They were about to go to a tournament, and Arthur was determined not to be left out. It was worth just one more try:

"I promise I won't get in the way, and I'll sharpen your weapons and shine up your armor and look after the horses," he said, trying a direct appeal to his father. Sir Ector, busy loading the saddlebags, did not look up.

"You can't go," said Kay dismissively. "You're not even a knight."

Kay, or rather *Sir* Kay, as Arthur now had to call him, had just been knighted, and took delight in reminding his brother of this fact at any opportunity. After years of training, he was, at last, allowed to take part in a real tournament. His sword was razor sharp, his new armor had been polished to perfection, and he could hardly wait to show off his jousting skills. The last thing he needed was his little brother tagging along.

"But you'll need a squire," said Arthur. "Please let me be your squire."

Sir Ector glanced down at Arthur's earnest, expectant face. There were good reasons why he didn't want him to go. He wished he could explain. But then, what harm could it really do?

"Well, Arthur, I suppose you might be useful. . . ."

"But father!" protested Kay. Ector ignored him.

"And you'll be a knight yourself soon, so this will be a chance for you to learn how to behave. But one hint of trouble—"

"You won't even know I'm there!" grinned Arthur. He was already packing his bag. Kay shot him a filthy look and was still muttering under his breath when they set off.

The tournament had been arranged for New Year's Day, and people were coming from far and wide to take part or watch. Knights with their squires, dukes and earls, ladies on horseback, barons with their servants, whole families of peasants, wandering minstrels, shepherds, beggars, butchers, bakers, candlestick-makers and hordes of other curious onlookers thronged the muddy road, all heading for the town where the tournament was to take place. Ector soon realized that they'd have little chance of finding a place to stay unless one of them went ahead.

"I'll go!" said Arthur. "I'll try the Blue Boar Inn first, and if there's no room there, I'll leave a message to say where I've gone."

"All right," said Ector. "We'll meet you there. Ride safely!"

Arthur charged off at full gallop, and

as soon as he was out of earshot, Ector turned to Kay conspiratorially.

"I think you should know that this isn't just any old tournament," he said.

"What do you mean?" asked Kay.

"Well, the story I've heard is that the Archbishop has arranged it for a particular purpose."

"And what's that?"

"To find the new king," said Ector.

Kay looked confused.

"Well, you know that since King Uther died ~ it must be over thirteen years ago now ~ the kingdom's been in complete chaos. There was no known successor to the throne, so all the knights and barons have been fighting among themselves. And to make matters worse, King Uther's old enemies have invaded parts of the kingdom." Ector paused and pulled his cloak around him. The afternoon air was growing colder as the weak winter sun began to set.

"Well, apparently," continued Ector, "an old sorcerer came out of his hiding place in Wales just before Christmas and told the Archbishop to summon all the nobles to a big service in the cathedral. He said there would be a miracle which would reveal the true heir to the throne. Well, the Archbishop adores miracles, so he did what the old sorcerer said.

"On Christmas morning, the nobles all packed into the cathedral. In fact, I've heard there wasn't enough room for

everybody inside, so some of them spilled out into the square. The service started and the Archbishop was about to give one of his long, boring sermons, when all of a sudden there was some shouting outside. Everybody immediately piled out into the square to see what all the noise was about." Ector stopped for a moment to read a milestone at the side of the road. They still had some way to go.

"And what was the noise about?" asked Kay impatiently.

"I'm just coming to that," said Ector. He spurred on his horse and then coughed to clear his throat.

"When they got outside they saw a strange block of stone, which had just appeared as if from nowhere. Sticking out of the stone was the handle of a very large sword. They all crowded around for a closer look and saw carved into the stone the message:

WHOEVER PULLS THIS SWORD OUT OF THIS STONE IS THE TRUEBORN KING OF LOGRES.

"Well, of course, all the knights started jostling to take turns to pull the sword out. One after another, they leaped up onto the block, heaving and straining, puffing and panting and moaning and groaning until they were red in the face. But not even the strongest knight could budge the sword an inch. It was as if the metal and the stone had been fused together.

"Well, finally

the Archbishop decided that the trueborn king was not there. And that was when he had the idea for this tournament ~ as a way of bringing all the nobles in the land together for jousting and to take a turn with the sword. That way he'd be sure to find the king. So he quickly chose some messengers to ride around the kingdom to tell people about the sword in the stone, and picked out ten knights to guard it."

"So. . . will I get the chance to pull the sword out?" asked Kay.

"Well, yes, if we can get anywhere near it with all this excitement," said Ector.

By now they were approaching the town walls. People were streaming in through the gates and surging along the narrow, cobbled streets. Ector and Kay made their way through the crowd to the cathedral square. A large mob had gathered around the stone, and the guards were letting knights through, one by one, to try to pull the sword out. Kay wanted to try immediately, but Ector stopped him.

"There'll be plenty of time for that tomorrow," he said. "Now we should see what Arthur's up to."

"He'd better have found us a place to stay," growled Kay.

Arthur didn't disappoint them. He'd managed to find some small rooms at the Blue Boar, which was only a couple of miles from the tournament ground. They ate some supper and went straight to bed. The tournament was due to start early the following morning.

Kay woke up feeling nervous ~ so nervous, in fact, that he forgot to put on his sword. He didn't discover this

until they were already well on their way to the tournament. He blamed Arthur and told him to ride back to get it.

Arthur galloped off at once. But when he arrived back at the inn, he found the heavy front door locked and bolted. He pounded on the wood with his fists, but no one answered. He went to each of the ground floor windows and yelled through the shutters, but there was no reply. Everybody had gone to the tournament.

"Where on earth am I going to get a sword from now?" he wailed miserably. "Kay will kill me if I go back without one."

Frustrated and despondent, he rode through the deserted town, and was still thinking about what to do when he passed in front of the cathedral. Something glinting in the sunlight caught his eye. He trotted over to investigate.

"The answer to my prayers!" he told himself, seeing a very large sword sticking out of a big block of stone. The square was empty. The guards had all abandoned their posts to go to the tournament.

Without bothering to stop and read the inscription, Arthur climbed up, grasped the handle of the sword in both hands and gave it a sharp tug. As smoothly and silently as a snake leaving its burrow, the shining blade slid from the stone.

Arthur stood for a moment, staring at his amazing find, before glancing around quickly to make sure he wasn't being watched. Then he leaped down and sliced the crisp morning air with the sparkling blade in a furious, imaginary fight. Then he remembered that the tournament was about to begin, so he hid the sword under his cloak and galloped back as fast as he could.

"Here's a sword!" he said, holding it out to Kay. "I couldn't get yours, but. . ."

Kay recognized the sword immediately, and before Arthur could finish his sentence he had snatched it from him, tucked it under his own cloak and rushed off to find Sir Ector.

"Look what I've done!" Kay said excitedly, when he found him. "It's the sword from the stone. I pulled it out! I must be the trueborn king!"

Sir Ector gave Kay a quizzical look.

"Well, if you can do it once, you can do it again, and this time you'll have an audience," he said calmly. He insisted that they all ride straight back to the cathedral, even though he knew that meant they would miss the tournament. And every time Arthur opened his mouth to try to tell Ector what had really happened, Kay silenced him with a menacing glare.

Back at the cathedral, Ector marched them straight over to the stone.

"Now, put the sword back exactly where you found it, Kay," he said. Kay jumped up onto the stone and tried to thrust the sword into it, but failed miserably.

"It's strange that you could pull it out, but you can't put it back," said Ector.

Kay climbed down, shamefaced.

"Now tell me where you really got it from," said Ector.

"From Arthur," admitted Kay, not daring to look his father in the eye.

"And where did _you_ get it from?" Ector asked patiently, turning to Arthur.

"From the stone, I promise," babbled Arthur. "I tried to get Kay's sword, but the door was locked, and. . . I knew he'd be cross, and I saw the sword and. . . I didn't want him to miss the tournament, so I took it and I. . ."

"Calm down, Arthur," said Ector. "Now let's see if you can put it back."

Arthur took the sword from Kay and climbed up onto the stone. The blade slid back in, like a warm knife into butter. Sir Ector then climbed up next to him and tried to pull it out. He failed.

"Now it's your turn, Kay," he said. Kay jumped up and seized the handle. He pulled and yanked and heaved but had no more luck than his father. Finally, Arthur, still unable to see what all the fuss was about, climbed up, grabbed the handle and once more effortlessly pulled the sword from the stone.

When he looked down, much to his surprise, his father and brother were

His father and brother were kneeling in front of him. . .

kneeling in front of him, their heads bowed.

"What are you doing?" he asked.

"Kneeling before our king," Ector replied. "Read the words on the stone, Arthur, and you'll see that there's only one person alive who can pull out this sword, and he's our trueborn king."

Arthur started to feel dizzy and slightly faint. He read the words over and over again until they swam in front of his eyes. It must be a mistake. . . or somebody was playing a trick on him. How could he be the king? He wasn't even a knight, nor from a royal family. His head started to spin. Then he felt a reassuring hand on his shoulder.

"Sit down, Arthur," said Ector. "There are a few things I need to tell you, but it's hard to know where to start."

"At the beginning?" suggested Arthur, sitting on a low wall.

"At the beginning," sighed Ector, as he sat down next to him. "This is going to be a shock for you, Arthur, but you had to know someday."

Ector took a deep breath, before launching into the story he'd been dreading having to tell...

"The night of your birth, Arthur, there was a terrible storm. Huge waves lashed the rocks, the wind howled and the roads became rivers overnight. I remember it well, because shortly after midnight there was a knock on the door. Outside, huddled against the biting wind, was a hunched, ragged figure, cradling something under his cloak. I knew exactly who he was and why he was there. It was Merlin, the sorcerer, disguised as a beggar, and the bundle he was carrying was a tiny, newborn child. He had climbed down the secret cliff path from Tintagel Castle, just before it was cut off by the tide, and scrambled along the beach in the driving rain. The baby, wrapped in a gold cloth, was the son of King Uther Pendragon and Duchess Igrayne."

Sir Ector paused for a moment to see how much of this story Arthur was taking in, but it was impossible to tell. The boy's head was lowered and his eyes were fixed firmly on his feet.

"You see, King Uther had a great many enemies and Merlin had told him that if the infant stayed at the castle, his young life would be in danger. So Merlin arranged to bring the baby to us in secret. He told us to raise him as our own son, and said that we should call him Arthur."

Sir Ector paused again. Arthur was staring at him with a puzzled look on his face.

"So I'm not really your son," he said slowly, in disbelief. "And Kay ~ he's not really my. . ." Ector quickly cut in:

"I didn't want to have to tell you this, Arthur. I've always thought of you as my own son. I tried to forget about what happened that night ~ though I knew the story would come out one day, when Merlin thought the time was right. When I heard about the sword in the stone, I did my best to stop you from finding out about it, but I knew the time had come. Merlin had arranged it."

"That's why I didn't want you to come with us. I couldn't bear to lose you. . ." His voice trailed off. It was Arthur's turn to speak:

"But, even if this is true, and I *am* the trueborn king, I'll always think of you as my father, and Kay will always be my brother ~ however mean he's been to me," he added.

There was a painfully long silence.

"What happened to my real mother and father?" Arthur asked, eventually.

"Your father was poisoned by one of his enemies when you were only two years old," said Ector solemnly, "but I believe your mother is still alive, and you have a sister, called Anna, and a half-sister."

There were still so many questions Arthur wanted to ask, but he had to wait. First they had to decide what to do about the sword. They made an appointment to see the Archbishop that same day to explain what had happened. As soon as he had seen Arthur removing the sword again, the Archbishop made an official announcement that the trueborn king had been found, and rushed off to get ready for the coronation.

Most of the knights roared with laughter when they heard that Arthur was heir to the throne, refusing to believe that this shy young man, who wasn't even a knight, could be their ruler. Only a few nobles who had survived from the days of King Uther, and who recognized the family likeness, swore their allegiance. The rest were scornful. They dispersed reluctantly, muttering that the whole thing had been fixed and that they'd never swear loyalty to this unknown upstart.

So the Archbishop had no choice but to arrange some more tournaments ~ four, in fact, for Twelfth Night, Candlemas, Easter and Whitsun, when once again, anyone who wanted could have a turn at removing the sword. On each occasion, of all the hundreds of knights, dukes, barons, earls and ordinary people who tried to remove the sword, only Arthur was successful.

At the Whitsun tournament, when he had accomplished the feat for the final time, a loud cheer went up from the huge crowd that had gathered to watch.

"We want Arthur!" someone shouted. "Arthur for king!" yelled another. Then a murmur started at the back of the crowd and the murmur grew to a rumble, and the rumble to a roar.

"WE WANT ARTHUR! WE WANT ARTHUR! WE WANT ARTHUR!" chanted the crowd, stamping their feet and drowning out the groans of a portly baron who had hauled himself onto the stone and was desperately straining to dislodge the sword. Shepherds were banging their crooks on the ground, tinkers were clanging their pots, children were clapping their hands, dogs were barking, and even the Archbishop found himself tapping his toes in time to the rhythm.

"WE WANT ARTHUR! WE WANT ARTHUR!" The huge uproar continued unabated, until at last even the most stubborn knights realized that, incredible as it might seem, Arthur must be their true and rightful king.

Row after row of knights, lords and ladies dropped to their knees to swear loyalty to Arthur, and begged his forgiveness for having delayed his succession for so long.

Arthur passed among them, shaking hands with them and accepting their apologies. When the clamor finally died down, the Archbishop stepped forward and announced that the king would be knighted immediately.

Arthur was carried jubilantly into the cathedral and people crammed the aisles to see the Archbishop knight him with the sword from the stone.

A few days later, King Arthur was crowned, amid rejoicing and celebration. The new king promised to rule justly over his people, to right all wrongs, to drive out the invaders, and to bring peace and prosperity to the troubled Kingdom of Logres.

After the ceremony, there was a noisy procession through the streets, with the crowds cheering their new leader along.

Unseen at the back of the crowd stood a mysterious, bearded figure in a long cloak.

At first, Arthur was unaware of him. But then, as if from nowhere, he suddenly heard a deep, resonant voice echoing inside his head:

"Many who scorn you
soon will serve you.
Many called friends will
one day be enemies.
Yours is a time of wonder,
a time of triumph,
a time of magic.
Rule wisely, King Arthur.
You are destined for
eternal greatness."

Arthur looked all around to see where the voice had come from, but Merlin had vanished into the night.

CHAPTER TWO

EXCALIBUR

King Arthur never forgot the solemn vow he made on the day he was crowned, but it was no easy task to bring peace to the Kingdom of Logres.

The land he now ruled had been torn apart by year after year of struggle and strife, and his father's old enemies seemed to be everywhere. His subjects were weary of long, bitter battles and worn down by the hardship and misery they had endured in those dark and troubled days.

Soon after his coronation, Arthur gathered an army and drove out the invaders. He restored all the stolen land to its rightful owners, and set about building castles to defend all the coasts and borders of the kingdom. As soon as this was done, he summoned his most loyal knights and followers and set up court at Camelot, the biggest and most beautiful castle in the whole of Logres.

It was at Camelot that he was finally reunited with his real mother, Igrayne, his sister, Anna, and his half-sister, Morgan le Fay, a powerful sorceress, who had learned all her magic from Merlin. Despite the joy and excitement of meeting his real family, Arthur didn't forget Ector and Kay. Each member of his foster family was given an honorary position in the new royal household.

One morning, about a year into Arthur's reign, a bedraggled squire rode into the courtyard at Camelot on a shambling horse. Hobbling behind him was another horse, with the bloodied body of the squire's master, Sir Miles, slumped across its saddle. The boy was so upset he could hardly speak, and it was some time before he had calmed down enough to explain what had happened.

He described how he and his master had been trotting through the forest when Sir Miles had been attacked by a knight called Sir Pellinore. Sir Pellinore was a formidable fighter. He liked nothing better than to boast about how many knights he had killed. And now he had set up his tent by a well near the road, and would not let anyone pass unless they jousted with him.

When the tearful young squire had finished this story, he flung himself to his knees and begged King Arthur to help him avenge the death of his master. Arthur, moved by the young man's plight, was considering what to do when Gryflet, a squire of the court, strode forward and volunteered to face Sir Pellinore himself.

"You're much too young, Gryflet," said

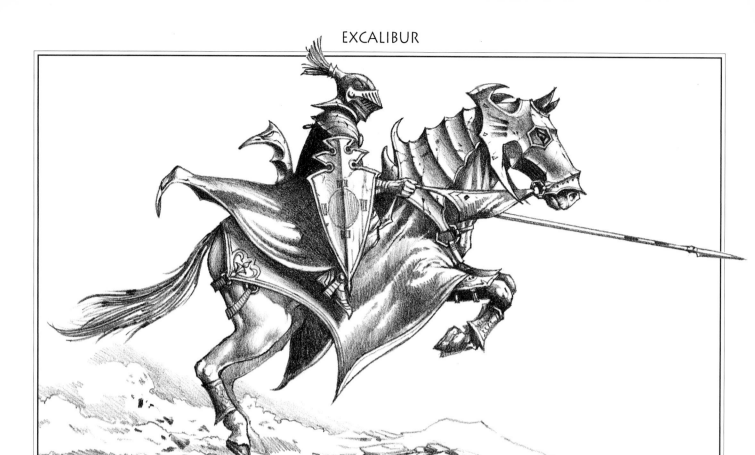

Arthur, "and no match for Sir Pellinore. You'll be an excellent knight when you're older, and I don't want to lose you now." But Gryflet continued to plead with such persistence that eventually Arthur relented. He told Gryflet that he would knight him and let him ride out to the forest only if he promised to joust with Pellinore just once, and then come straight back to Camelot.

Gryflet eagerly agreed, and quickly knelt down to be knighted. Then he put on his armor, seized his weapons and charged across the drawbridge. But in no time he was back, clinging feebly to his horse's neck, with a deep spear wound in his side.

Arthur was furious. By the time a surgeon arrived, he was galloping out of the gates himself, fully armed and with his heart set on revenge.

When he reached the edge of the forest, a boy of about fourteen suddenly stepped out into the road in front of him.

"Whoa!" yelled the boy, raising his hand. Arthur brought his horse to an abrupt halt.

"Why do you look so serious?" asked the boy with a cheeky grin.

"Because of the things I've seen," said Arthur, surprised by the question.

"I know that already," snapped the boy. "In fact, I know everything you're thinking and I know that you're a fool." Arthur could hardly believe his ears, but the boy went on undaunted:

"And I know your mother and I knew your father, King Uther, and. . ."

"You little liar!" yelled Arthur. "You've got no idea what you're talking about. You're far too young to know any of this. Now get out of my sight!"

The boy sidled off into the forest, and almost at once an old man wearing a long purple cloak appeared in his place. His face looked kind and wise.

"Why do you look so serious, Sir?" the old man asked in a sonorous voice.

Not again, thought Arthur.

"Because I've just met a cheeky boy who called me a fool and said that he knew my father," was his reply.

"But he *did* know your father," insisted the old man. "And he knows many other things about you. He knows that one day your kingdom will fall to a child who is not yet born, and that the same child will grow up to kill you in battle, and that the child will be named Mordred, and..."

"Stop!" said Arthur. "Who are you to tell me all of this?"

"Merlin," said the old man, and before Arthur's eyes he changed back into the boy and vanished into thin air with an eerie little laugh that rang through the forest.

"Merlin!" called Arthur. "Come back! I need to talk to you!" But Merlin had gone.

Arthur had heard countless stories about Merlin. He even recognized his voice, but it was the first time they'd met face to face, since the day he was born.

He continued slowly along the road, pondering the prophecies Merlin had made. He hadn't gone much further when he saw the old man again, sprinting frantically through the trees, his cloak billowing behind him. Hard on his heels ran three evil-looking thugs.

Arthur charged after them, brandishing his sword and shouting at the top of his voice. The thugs bolted into the forest.

"Your magic couldn't save you this time," said Arthur.

"It could have done," the sorcerer replied casually, not even pausing for breath, "more than your anger will save you when you meet Sir Pellinore."

Merlin mounted his horse, which was grazing at the side of the road, and accompanied Arthur on his journey to face Sir Pellinore. Arthur fired questions at him all the way, but Merlin refused to answer. When they reached the well, they saw Sir Pellinore, fully armed and grim faced, sitting on a huge horse in front of his tent. Arthur gulped, suddenly feeling very nervous.

"Sir Pellinore..?" he asked hesitantly. The menacing figure said nothing.

"Sir Pellinore," Arthur repeated, "I've been told that you're stopping people from passing along this road."

Pellinore turned slowly in his saddle and fixed Arthur with a belligerent stare.

"That's true," he said tersely.

"Well, I've come to demand that you change your ways," said Arthur, trying to sound important and doing his best to disguise the wobble in his voice.

"You'll just have to force me, then, won't you?" said Sir Pellinore, gripping his lance and turning his horse around, ready to joust.

Sighing, Arthur clapped down his visor. This knight was obviously not in the mood for a discussion.

They jousted three times, charging fearlessly across the clearing and clashing their lances together. The horses panted and steamed as their sharp hooves pounded the dewy grass into mud. The first and second time, both of the lances broke and neither knight could gain an advantage. But the third time the opponents clashed together, Sir Pellinore swung his lance into exactly the right position, and Arthur was knocked off his horse. He leaped to his feet, abandoned his lance and whipped his sword from its scabbard.

"You may be better at jousting," he shouted bravely, "but let's see what you can do on foot."

Pellinore dismounted. Reluctant though he was to relinquish the advantage he had gained on horseback, the rules of chivalry had to be obeyed.

They fought long and hard until both of them collapsed, breathless with pain and exhaustion. Their armor was dented, and blood trickled onto the grass, but neither fighter would give in.

Merlin leaned on his staff at the edge of the clearing, watching impassively as the two men staggered to their feet and the fighting started again. Once more the clash of swords and the groans of the duelers echoed through the forest, until

Arthur's sword snapped in two.

"Surrender or die!" panted Pellinore.

"Never!" screamed Arthur, dropping the broken sword. He rushed at Pellinore full tilt, grabbed him around the waist and knocked him down to the ground. Pellinore fought like a wild cat to release himself, until, with a blood-curdling cry, he overturned Arthur, climbed on top of him and pinned him down on the grass.

Arthur stared up into the big knight's frenzied face, struggling desperately to free himself from the vice-like grip of his enemy. But he wasn't strong enough.

Pellinore wrenched off Arthur's helmet, raised his heavy sword

above his head, and was just about to bring the blade down on Arthur's neck to deliver the fatal blow, when Merlin muttered a hasty spell.

Pellinore's eyes clamped shut. His sword fell from his hand and he toppled slowly forward.

"Have you killed him?" asked Arthur breathlessly, easing himself out from under the lifeless body. "Is he dead?"

"No," replied the magician, casually prodding the body with his staff. "He's just asleep. Actually he's in much better shape than you are." Arthur by now was slumped on the ground, moaning, and bleeding badly from several wounds.

"You're going to need good fighters like him, and he'll live to serve you well," said Merlin. "His son Percival is going to be one of the bravest Knights of the Round Table."

Arthur was too weak and exhausted to take any of this in, or to ask the sorcerer what he meant. Merlin helped him climb onto his horse, and they set off again into the woods, leaving Sir Pellinore lying on the muddy grass, among the wreckage of broken weapons and armor.

Merlin led the way to a cottage deep in the forest which was the home of an ancient healer. The old man treated Arthur's wounds with herbal lotions, and after three days he was well enough to ride again. They thanked the healer and left.

"I wish I hadn't broken my sword," said Arthur as they were riding through the forest.

"Don't worry," said Merlin, "you'll soon have another that will last for ever. It'll be the best sword in the world, forged in the depths of Lake Avalon."

Arthur had no idea what Merlin was talking about. But the old magician always seemed to know exactly what was going to happen, so he said nothing. And at that moment, they trotted out of the shadow of the trees into bright sunshine. A gleaming expanse of water lay before them, with a huge, purple mountain rising up behind it.

Arthur scanned the lake's silvery surface, and without knowing why, he found his eyes coming to rest on a spot in the middle. Without any warning, a hand suddenly shot up from beneath the water, holding a jewel-covered sword and scabbard, which sparkled in the sunlight.

"Look over there!" shouted Arthur in amazement. "Look at that sword!"

"That's Excalibur, Arthur. It's the sword you will carry to the end of your days."

Arthur had jumped down from his saddle and was wading into the water as if drawn to the sword by some magical force. A fine mist was rolling down the mountainside and rapidly covering the lake.

"Look," said Merlin, pointing across the water. A tall woman in a long robe was gliding across the surface toward them.

"That's the Lady of the Lake," Merlin whispered. "If you want Excalibur, you must do exactly what she says."

The Lady of the Lake was now right in front of them, hovering just above the still, misty water. Arthur stared at her in disbelief.

"King Arthur," she said in a deep, gentle voice, "Excalibur will be yours if you agree

"Look over there!" shouted Arthur in amazement.

"Look at that sword!"

to do whatever I ask in the future."

"I will do whatever it is in my power to do," said Arthur, intent only on getting hold of the sword as soon as possible. "I promise," he added hurriedly.

"Then use my barge," said the Lady, gesturing toward an ornate boat, half-hidden among the reeds.

Arthur needed no more encouragement. He raced along the shore, stepped into the boat and pushed out into the deep, dark water. The barge drifted silently across the lake, parting the carpet of mist before it. When it reached the middle, Arthur stretched out and plucked the sword and scabbard from the fairy hand. At once, the little arm disappeared back into the water.

Excalibur was the most beautiful weapon Arthur had ever seen. He was so lost in admiration that he was unaware of the boat floating gently back to the shore, or of the Lady of the Lake vanishing into the still water. By the time he looked back, the surface was as smooth and calm as before.

Merlin and Arthur started back through the forest. When they reached the well, they saw the mighty Sir Pellinore lying asleep, just as they had left him. But all of his wounds were now healed.

"I won't wake him just yet," said Merlin, "though I can guarantee he won't give you any more trouble."

"That's a shame," replied Arthur, "because now I have Excalibur, I'd like to fight him again, and this time I'd win."

"Don't be so sure," said Merlin wisely, shaking his head at the young king's haste. "He's still a stronger fighter than you are. Anyway, there'll be plenty of opportunity to use Excalibur very soon indeed."

Arthur drew the sword out of its scabbard once more, so that he could admire it again.

"Which of them do you like best?" asked Merlin. "The sword itself, or the scabbard?"

"The sword, definitely," said Arthur, gazing in awe at the heavy, razor sharp silver blade, and tracing with his fingers the strange patterns carved into the sword's jewel-covered hilt.

"Then you're a fool," said Merlin bluntly, "because the scabbard is enchanted, and it's worth much more than the sword. While you're wearing that scabbard, you'll never lose a drop of blood, however badly you're injured."

"That's the second time you've called me a fool," Arthur pointed out, although he realized that what Merlin had just told him made the sword even more precious than he had imagined.

Their horses were now trudging up a slope on the final approach to Camelot, and the sun was just setting.

"Well, I may be a fool," the king announced at last, grinning at Merlin, "but now I'm a fool with the best sword in the world!"

Then, laughing with excitement and holding Excalibur high in the air, he spurred on his horse to gallop the last stretch home to Camelot.

CHAPTER THREE

THE GATHERING OF THE KNIGHTS

Merlin sighed, folded his arms and looked straight into Arthur's face.

"You're making a mistake," he said slowly and solemnly. "A *big* mistake."

Arthur had just told the ancient sorcerer that he wanted to marry Guinevere, the beautiful daughter of King Leodegrance.

"But I—" protested Arthur. Merlin cut in sharply:

"I know she's probably the most charming and beautiful woman you've ever met, and you no doubt believe that you're in love with her, but it's exactly that which will bring about the destruction of all that is important to you. I beg you to think again. Does it have to be Guinevere?"

"Yes," said Arthur defiantly, "it does."

Arthur rode to Leodegrance's castle at once to propose to Guinevere, and the lovely princess accepted without hesitation. Her father was overjoyed at the prospect of having the King of Logres as a son-in-law, so Arthur announced their wedding plans immediately.

All the knights and ladies in the kingdom were invited to the celebrations. After the wedding, they lined up across the courtyard at Camelot to welcome the king and his new bride home. A rousing fanfare sounded, and the massive doors of the hall swung open to reveal Merlin, standing in front of the most enormous round table.

"Welcome, royal King and Queen of Logres!" said the sorcerer. "What you see before you is your wedding present from King Leodegrance. It has been in his family for many generations, but it is your rightful inheritance. Use it wisely."

Arthur and Guinevere gazed in awe at the extraordinary spectacle. The guests crowded in behind them in silent amazement. Spread out on the colossal table was an elaborate meal ~ huge raised pies and whole roasted swans, peacocks, woodcocks, pheasants and quails, great slabs of venison, succulent wild boar, pasties and puddings and mustard and mead, vast jugs of ale and ruby red wine, lampreys and eels and spit-roasted ox, frumenty, dumplings, sweet cherry pies, all laid out together as a feast for their eyes.

But compared to the table itself, the banquet seemed almost insignificant. Around the immense table top there was space for dozens of people to sit comfortably. The finely polished oak surface was inlaid with intricate coats of arms. Each of the table's legs was as thick as a tree trunk, carved with beautiful birds and animals and intertwined leaves and flowers. Every one of the golden seats was upholstered with the finest tapestry.

The king and queen walked majestically all around the huge circumference, running their hands over the glistening wood, admiring the marquetry and inspecting the seats one by one. On the back of each seat was inscribed a name: SIR BALAN, SIR KAY, SIR URIENS, SIR UWAIN, SIR BALYN, SIR MELLIGRANCE, SIR AGRAVAIN, SIR PELLINORE, SIR LAUNFAL, SIR BEDIVERE ~ names well known to Arthur; SIR PERCIVAL, SIR LANCELOT ~ names he did not even recognize; SIR GAWAIN and SIR TOR ~ squires who were not yet knights ~ and many more besides.

"When a knight dies, or is killed in battle, his name shall slowly fade and disappear," explained Merlin, "until a new knight comes to replace him."

"Well, I think my name looks quite healthy at the moment!" the king joked, passing his own seat, which was the grandest of all.

At that moment Sir Pellinore, Arthur's old enemy, strode in through the door, followed by his son, Tor.

"At your humble service, my king," they both said, to Arthur's

astonishment, bowing deeply before taking their places at the table.

When everyone was seated, Arthur summoned Tor, along with his own nephew, Gawain, to be knighted. Then he and Guinevere found their own seats and looked around at the familiar smiling faces. Only the places for Sir Lancelot and Sir Percival were empty.

Arthur banged on the table to get everyone's attention.

"No more arguments about who sits where!" he announced. "All shall be equal at this table. No single knight is more important than another. From today, you shall all be known as the Knights of the Round Table, the bravest and most noble knights in the world. Your fame will spread across the kingdom and across the seas to lands far away. Stories of your adventures will be passed from one generation to the next, down the centuries. Now raise your goblets and let us drink to the future."

"To the future!" cried the knights, holding their wine goblets high in the air.

"To King Arthur and Queen Guinevere!" called out Sir Pellinore.

"And to all the Knights of the Round Table!" added Merlin.

Everyone joined in the toast, and

drank deeply to their king and their fellow knights. Then the babble of excited voices echoed around the hall and out across the courtyard as the celebrations began.

Exactly one year and many adventures later, the knights were once more gathered around the table when a trumpet sounded in the courtyard. Into the hall rode the Lady of the Lake, followed by three young squires. The tallest of them had flowing golden hair, broad shoulders and a warm, winning smile.

"I have come on Merlin's orders," said the Lady, "to present to you Lancelot du Lake, my foster-son. I have brought him up in my palace in Lake Avalon. When I gave you Excalibur you promised that you would do whatever I asked in the future. Well now I have come to make a request. I entrust Lancelot to you. I ask that you make him a Knight of the Round Table."

Queen Guinevere's face had turned as white as a sheet. She stared at the handsome young newcomer, as if awestruck. Not noticing, King Arthur stepped forward graciously to greet him.

"Welcome to Camelot, Lancelot," said Arthur. "Your place awaits you at the table, but who are these other squires?"

"Hector and Lionel," said the Lady of the Lake. "Their seats are ready too."

Arthur turned back to face the table. In the year since his wedding celebrations, two of his knights had died. The names "SIR LIONEL" and "SIR HECTOR" were rapidly forming on the backs of the empty seats. Arthur drew his sword and gestured to the three squires to kneel before him. Lancelot was last to be knighted.

"Arise, Sir Lancelot du Lake," said Arthur. Lancelot got to his feet, strode over to Guinevere and bowed deeply, before taking his place at the table. His brown eyes twinkled in the candlelight. His broad, warm smile revealed flashing white teeth. Guinevere smiled back.

"Greetings, good knight," she said breathlessly, scarcely able to conceal the tremble in her voice.

From that day on, Lancelot vowed to serve and protect Queen Guinevere. Over the years he won more tournaments and battles and survived more dangerous quests than any other knight in the kingdom, and soon he became Arthur's closest friend and most trusted ally. But his love for Guinevere grew stronger and stronger. Not one of the clever and charming princesses or beautiful young women that he met on his travels meant anything to him. Queen Guinevere was his only true love.

Sir Percival came to Camelot a few years later, by a very different route. He was brought up in the forests of Wales, never knowing his father. In fact, apart from his mother, he knew no one except animals, birds, trees, the wind and the water until the age of sixteen.

One day, he was wandering alone in the forest as usual, when five knights came riding by. Their armor sparkled in the sunshine and their bridles jingled as they trotted through the trees.

"Arise, Sir Lancelot du Lake."

"Good morning, young man," said Lancelot when he saw the boy.

Percival was dumbstruck. He had never seen such a sight.

"Don't look so amazed," laughed another of the knights. "We won't bite!"

"Are you angels?" ventured the wide-eyed Percival, trembling with nervousness. "My mother's told me about angels," he added.

"Mere mortals, I'm afraid," laughed the knight, "on our way to Camelot."

"We're Knights of the Round Table," explained Sir Lancelot kindly. "We serve King Arthur of Logres."

"Perhaps you could be a knight too, one day," said one of the other knights.

"But how do I do that?" asked Percival eagerly.

"By proving yourself worthy," said the knight. Then they cantered off through the forest.

This chance encounter was enough to stir Percival to action. He went straight home and told his mother that the next day he was going away to Camelot to become a Knight of the Round Table. His mother sighed deeply and cried a little, but she did not try to stop him. Merlin had warned her that this was her son's destiny. She also knew that Percival's father, Sir Pellinore, was now a famous knight. Their son had obviously inherited his father's taste for adventure.

Percival was true to his word. Barefoot, dressed in animal skins and armed only with a hunting knife, he set off the very next day. He trudged through the forest, sleeping among gnarled tree roots, drinking from streams and eating only nuts and berries, until he came to the great white road that led to Camelot. By the time he reached the castle his feet were raw and his legs were aching, but he did not waver from his task.

By mingling with a group of servants, he managed to sneak in through the castle gates. Then he made his way toward the great hall where the knights were eating their supper. As he stood nervously in the shadows, he saw a large man dressed in golden armor stride in through the door, snatch the golden goblet that King Arthur was drinking from, and march out into the night.

Arthur was furious. The knights clamored to be allowed to retrieve the cup, but the king would hear none of it.

"This is a trifling matter," he said, "not a quest worthy of a Knight of the Round Table. It's only a cup, after all. Some squire should go. If he can get the cup back, and returns wearing the golden armor, I'll reward him by making him a knight."

Percival saw his chance.

"I'll go!" he cried, jumping out of the shadows. All eyes turned toward the strange, scruffy youth.

"I'll get your cup ~ and the golden armor as well," Percival went on. "I'll be needing some anyway."

"Hah!" scoffed Sir Kay rudely. "How could a pathetic swineherd like you challenge a knight! Look at you, you're not even strong enought to *wear* his armor, let alone fight for it!"

"What's your name, young man?" asked Arthur, ignoring his foster-brother.

"Percival, Sir," came the confident answer. "And I'll get your cup, you'll see."

"You'll need a horse," said Arthur, recognizing the name from the empty seat at the table, "and a good meal by the looks of it, but I'll let you have a try."

So Percival was given his chance to prove himself, and Arthur was not disappointed. Three days later, the young man returned, looking very different from the ragged boy he had been. To everyone's amazement, he was dressed in the golden armor, carrying the stolen goblet and looking every inch the knight he was soon to become.

With one accurate throw of his hunting knife through a tiny chink in the golden knight's armor, Percival had managed to fell the huge warrior and then swipe the golden goblet from his saddlebag. He had achieved his quest and proved himself worthy, and his place awaited him at the Round Table.

Over the years that followed, the Knights of the Round Table grew famous far and wide for their amazing adventures, brave battles and skillful feats. With their help, Arthur

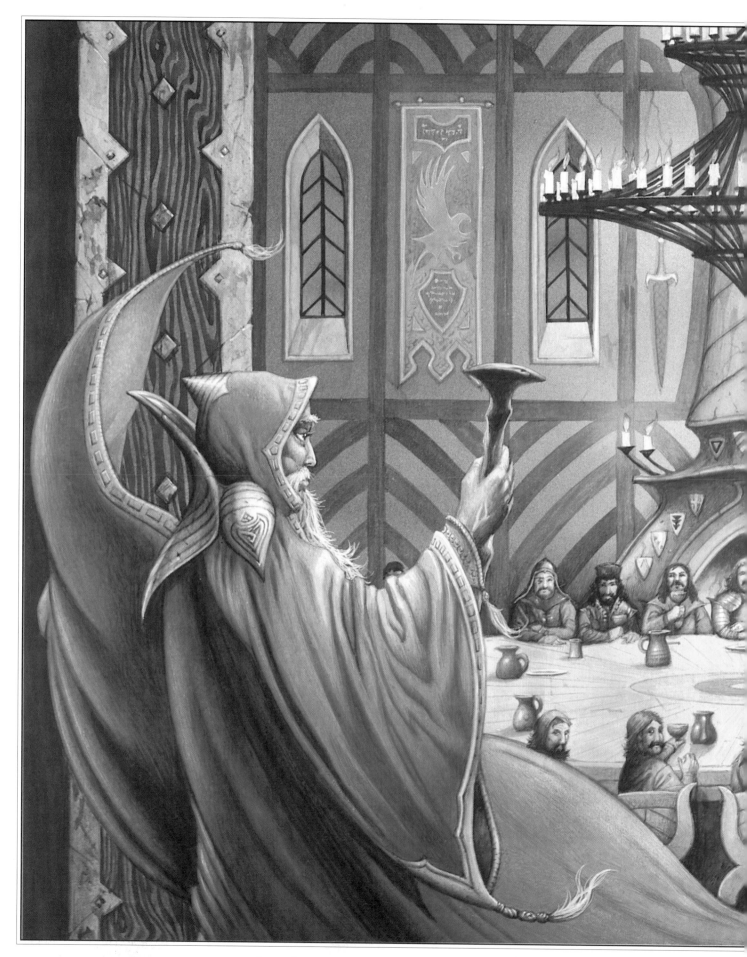

In the doorway stood Merlin. . . .

. . . with his cloak billowing out behind him in the stormy evening air.

was able to defend and strengthen his kingdom, defeating any attackers and invaders with ease. At long last, peace had arrived in Logres: the people were happy, the laws were kept, the land prospered, and it seemed that Arthur's realm would never again be torn apart by the terrors of war.

But although Arthur was a wise and thoughtful king, and his knights were the strongest and bravest fighters the world had ever known, not even they could control for ever the forces of evil that threatened them. Although they did not yet realize it, it was not outside the kingdom, but within its boundaries, that the worst danger lay.

One evening, after another long and delicious supper, Arthur gazed around the huge circular table with satisfaction. Almost every seat was taken, and as the king looked from one of his knights to another, his heart filled with pride and happiness to think how many wonderful followers and loyal friends he now had.

Who would have thought, he wondered, that after such a humble childhood he should end up like this, wealthy, powerful and content?

He was even lucky enough to have a beautiful wife, Arthur thought proudly to himself, and he reached for Guinevere's hand. He decided that he must always try to rule all his knights and subjects as well as they served him.

At that exact moment, the door of the great hall slowly creaked open. In the doorway stood Merlin, framed against the angry darkening sky, with his cloak billowing out behind him in the stormy evening air. He raised his long wooden staff and struck it three times on the stone floor.

As he did so the chatter in the hall gradually died down, the friendly clinking of cutlery subsided, and everyone turned around in their seats to listen to what the wise wizard had to say.

"Greetings, good knights," Merlin roared, and his old, croaking voice seemed to contain a hint of sadness and regret. Everyone in the hall, from the king himself to the merest servant waiting at the tables, maintained a respectful silence.

"I come to bring you encouragement and strength," Merlin went on mysteriously, "but also to warn you. Be on your guard, Knights of the Round Table. Danger can lurk around any corner. He who seems your friend may be your enemy. Do not let pride become your downfall."

Arthur felt a cold chill through his bones and shuddered slightly, clutching his wife's hand a little tighter. How did Merlin always seem to know what he was thinking? Just a moment ago he had been feeling proud and complacent about his good fortune. Now he had been reminded that a good knight must never become self-satisfied ~ and a king, despite his power and high position, must be even more careful to guard against pride.

He was about to ask the sorcerer to explain, but before he could do so, the heavy hall door swung closed. Merlin was gone.

CHAPTER FOUR

THE CURSED SWORD

After Merlin had warned the Round Table that danger lay ahead, all the knights were extra vigilant for a while. But nothing unusual seemed to happen, and they could see no reason not to continue adventuring, questing and jousting as before.

Arthur sometimes worried about exactly what kind of danger the ancient magician could have meant. But he had no idea. All he could do was to rule his kingdom as well as possible until Merlin's strange message became clear.

One evening a few months later, the castle kitchens were bustling with activity. All the knights who weren't away on adventures had spent a hard day practicing their jousting skills, and now a delicious aroma of roasting and baking wafted into the hall as their meal was prepared. Servants began to stream in, carrying silver platters of food and flagons of fine wine.

"Well then," announced the king, as he did every evening. "A good appetite and good health to all of you!"

The knights were just about to raise their goblets when there was a strange clattering noise. Everyone turned to look.

There, struggling in the doorway, was a young maiden. She was very beautiful, and wore a gorgeous green dress trimmed with gold. But she was lumbered with a huge, heavy sword, which seemed to be attached to her waist. It was much too long for her, so that the tip of its beautiful engraved scabbard scraped noisily along the stone tiles.

King Arthur stood up politely. "Damsel," he said, "welcome to Camelot. May we be of assistance to you in any way?"

"My lady has sent me here with a challenge," panted the maiden, "for a noble knight. This sword is fastened to me by magic. Only a true, pure-hearted and loyal knight, without treason or treachery, will be able to pull it out of its scabbard." She looked around the table.

"Well, you'll have no problem here," Arthur reassured her. "To set an example, I'll be the first to try." He went over to where the maiden stood, took hold of the sword's silver handle, and pulled.

He pulled harder.

Finally he pulled so hard that the maiden almost fell over.

"There's no need to yank it like that," she told the king. "In the right hands, it will come out easily."

So all the knights lined up to try to pull the sword out of its scabbard. But even knights who were famous for their bravery and good deeds ~ Sir Gaheris, Sir Bedivere, even Sir Lancelot ~ could not shift the maiden's sword a single inch.

The last knight in line was Sir Balyn. He was a quiet, shy knight, and had never really had a proper adventure. He was desperate to show Arthur that he was loyal and worthy. Only the week before, his brother Balan had set off on his first quest. Perhaps, Balyn thought, if he could pull out the sword, Arthur would send him on a quest too.

By now, most of the knights had wandered back to their seats, and the maiden stared at Balyn disdainfully.

"I don't think so," she said rudely as he approached. "If they couldn't do it, what chance have *you* got?"

"But I *am* a loyal and true knight," Balyn protested, a little hurt. "You can't always tell

someone's strengths just by looking at them, you know."

"Oh, go on, then," said the maiden, a little more kindly. And Balyn stepped forward and drew out the long sword in one smooth, graceful movement.

At the sight of the silver blade gleaming in the air, the king looked up. Some of the knights, stirred with jealousy, came to see what was going on.

Balyn himself, however, had suddenly started to feel very peculiar.

He was dizzy, and his vision was blurred. He could hear voices around him ~ King Arthur saying "Well done, Balyn!" and the maiden saying "This is truly a pure and loyal knight, and he will have many great adventures!"

But to Sir Balyn, they all seemed very strange and far away. And as he gripped the sword's hilt, carved with intertwining silver leaves, he felt himself filling up with a strange, unfamiliar sense of fear and burning anger.

"And now, Sir Balyn, I must return to my lady," the maiden was saying. "Give me the sword, please."

Balyn stared at her blankly.

"Give her the sword back, Balyn," said Arthur jovially. "Our food will be getting cold!"

"NO!" shouted Balyn suddenly, with a fury that surprised everyone in the great hall, including himself. His vision gradually cleared, and he looked around at the rows of shocked faces.

"The sword is mine now," said Balyn coldly. "I will not give it back."

"That's *not* a very good idea," warned the maiden. "You see, that sword won't bring you good luck. In fact, if you keep it, it will bring about your death. And with it, you'll kill your closest friend."

"I'll just have to take a chance on that, won't I?" answered Balyn arrogantly, hardly listening to the maiden. He didn't know where these words were coming from. He seemed to have suffered some kind of sudden personality change.

The maiden tried to persuade Balyn again, but he clung on to the sword, and looked so furious that no one wanted to argue with him. Eventually the maiden gave up, and ran from the castle, weeping.

"I'm going on an adventure," Balyn announced, and went to prepare his horse.

No sooner had Balyn left the great hall, than another lady appeared in the doorway. But this time it was a lady Arthur recognized ~ the tall, elegant Lady of the Lake. She had given Arthur his precious sword, Excalibur, and brought his best knight, Sir Lancelot, to Camelot.

Arthur wondered when he was ever going to get his dinner.

"King Arthur!" called the Lady of the Lake, in her deep, imposing voice. "I've come to ask you for another request."

"Of course, my lady," said Arthur. "What is your wish?"

"I want Sir Balyn's head," replied the Lady of the Lake.

Arthur stared at her in horror. Then he remembered that when she had given him Excalibur, he had promised to do anything she asked, whenever she asked him.

But this time Arthur would have to say no. He could not bring himself to kill Balyn, even if he was behaving a little oddly. And why would the Lady of the Lake make such a strange request?

"I'm sorry," said Arthur awkwardly, "but I can't agree to that."

"Do as I ask," said the Lady, wisely. "You won't regret it. I know what's best for you, Arthur, and I'm telling you, Balyn must die. He is a threat to your kingdom."

Just then, a shadow darkened the door behind the Lady. It was Balyn, gripping the hilt of the strange sword, and staring around the hall, grimacing horribly.

"So, you'd have me dead, would you?" he growled viciously, advancing slowly toward the Lady of the Lake. Suddenly, the sword in his hand swung upward and cut through the air, almost as if it was moving by itself, and before anyone could do anything to stop him, Balyn had sliced off the Lady's head.

Everyone gasped in amazement. The servants screamed, Sir Kay fainted, and Balyn sank to his knees, spattered with blood, gazing in horror at what he had done.

"For shame!" cried King Arthur, pushing back his chair and standing up angrily. "What possessed you to do this, Balyn? You have disgraced the Round Table ~ this lady was my friend, and she was unarmed and innocent!"

"I'm sorry. . . I. . . I didn't mean to—" sobbed Balyn. Still dragging the blood-stained sword, he picked himself up off the floor and backed away toward the door. "I'll make it up to you, my king," he choked, desperate for forgiveness.

"I don't care *what* you do," said Arthur, with deadly fury. "Just leave. Leave my castle and my court. And don't come back!"

"A terrible shame," said a wistful voice in Arthur's ear.

"Merlin!" Arthur found the ancient wizard standing at his shoulder.

"Terrible," the old magician repeated, his wise old eyes sparkling sadly. "Balyn would have been an excellent knight. Now, thanks to that sword, he's destined to bring misery to the whole kingdom. And unfortunately, he himself is doomed."

And with that, the wizened old sorcerer faded away into a tiny wisp of smoke.

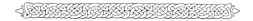

Out in the forest, Balyn rode fast and furiously. Every second carried him further away from Camelot, the scene of his awful crime. He was determined to make amends for what he had done, but how?

It began to rain softly, and Balyn was thinking about finding a place to rest for the night when he heard a shout behind him.

"Balyn! H*ey*! Sir Balyn! Come and fight me, you pathetic coward!"

Balyn turned his horse. In the distance, through the bleary rain, he could see a knight following him on a large black stallion. It was Sir Launceor, an Irish Knight of the Round Table. He was probably seeking vengeance for the Lady of the Lake, so as to get into Arthur's good books.

"What do you want from me, Launceor?" Balyn cried out. "Please ~ keep away from me, I'm bad luck. I don't want to fight."

"Coward," snarled Sir Launceor again, stopping a few feet away from Balyn. "Why don't you fight like a man, if you're so dangerous, instead of killing innocent women? Come on, let's see what you're made of!" He pulled down the visor on his helmet and pointed his lance at Balyn.

"I said NO," Balyn shouted. But it was too late. Sir Launceor was already backing off, ready to charge at him.

The two knights thundered toward each other, and crashed together with an almighty clang. Sir Launceor's lance hit the middle of Balyn's shield and splintered into a thousand pieces, and both knights were flung from their horses. They picked themselves up and reached for their swords.

When Balyn felt the heavy weight of the sword, the silver leaves on its hilt resting in his hand, he suddenly burned with vicious anger and hatred for Sir Launceor. Before the Irish knight could even get his weapon out of its scabbard, Balyn leapt forward and thrust the point of the sword into his stomach. The blade pierced the armor easily and Lanceor toppled to the ground. Balyn then drove the blade through his opponent's body, until he could feel it sticking into the springy turf underneath.

Launceor arched back on the grass with a gurgling groan. His helmet rolled off and Balyn gasped in horror at his open, staring eyes. Launceor was dead.

"No!" screamed a female voice. "No! Oh, Launceor, my love!"

A young woman, who had obviously been following Sir Launceor at a distance, came hurtling along the track and threw herself onto the dead man's body, kissing his face and crying hysterically. Then she began to pull at the sword that was pinning him to the ground.

"Don't!" Balyn shouted urgently. "Don't touch it!" But the lady would not listen. She heaved at the sword, tugging and jerking until she eventually managed to drag it out of Launceor's body by placing one foot on his stomach to steady herself, while Balyn tried uselessly to intervene.

"I can't live without him!" she cried, and before Balyn could stop her, she used the sword to slash her own throat. She fell down, flopping into the arms of her dead knight. The bloodstained sword toppled over, eventually coming to rest across the bodies of the two lovers.

Balyn sank down, appalled, onto the wet grass. What was happening? Everything he did seemed to lead to death and destruction. He thought he should throw the sword away, and yet ~ he couldn't.

He stared at the silver hilt until the swirling patterns of leaves began to make him dizzy. He wiped the blade on the grass, and fitted the weapon reluctantly back into its scabbard. Something told him it was his destiny to carry that sword until his dying day.

If only, thought Balyn miserably, if *only* my brother Sir Balan was here to help.

Balan was his best friend in the whole world. Since he had left on his quest, Balyn had missed him terribly. Balan was brave, clever and kind. He would know what to do.

In fact, thought Balyn sadly, Balan was a much better knight than he was.

After spending the night miserably in a cave, Balyn tried to continue his journey.

He hadn't made a very promising start, but he was still determined to do some good deeds to try to make up for what had happened to the Lady of the Lake ~ and now to poor Sir Launceor as well. Surely, Balyn thought, he must be able to use the power of the sword to help someone.

He had been traveling for most of the day when a tall, wizened old man wearing a long purple cloak appeared before him, holding up a gnarled hand.

"Merlin?" asked Balyn nervously. He felt terribly guilty.

"Balyn," said Merlin kindly. "I think it's time I told you what's going on."

"So do I," said Balyn.

"You're not going to like it," said Merlin, "but I'm afraid there's nothing to be done." He took a deep breath.

"When you pulled that sword out of its scabbard," the magician explained, "you brought a curse upon yourself ~ one that is centuries old. Whoever owns the sword becomes an evil monster, destined to terrify his comrades and bring about his own downfall. And also, whoever carries the sword shall kill—"

He looked sadly at Balyn. He couldn't bear to tell him.

". . . lots of people," he said at last.

Balyn looked bewildered. "But why?" he asked. He didn't want to cause all this death and destruction ~ all he wanted to do was to do some good deeds. "Who did this to me? Why would anyone want to harm the Round Table?"

"I tried to warn you," Merlin said sadly. "Someone is plotting against Arthur and the Knights of the Round Table ~ someone whose powers even I cannot overcome. And she will—"

Merlin broke off suddenly. He seemed to be listening intently, and eventually Balyn heard footsteps in the undergrowth, and the clinking of a sword.

"Balyn," Merlin continued, "it is too late to save you. But if, as I believe, you would like to use your power to do some good, I think there is someone nearby who needs your help. Follow him, Sir Balyn. And do your best. Good luck."

Merlin's voice was already fading away as he disappeared into the air.

Balyn stared, shocked and frightened, at the spot where the magician had stood. He didn't want to believe all that Merlin had told him, so he tried to put it out of his mind. He decided he had better take Merlin's last piece of advice, though, so he looked around to see who the magician had meant.

Suddenly, Balyn realized that he didn't know where he was. The landscape was unfamiliar, the trees were gnarled and stunted, and the wind was cold. The only sign of life was the irregular clinking, rustling sound Merlin had pointed out.

Following the sound, Balyn soon caught up with a knight limping weakly through the forest, tears streaming down his face. But when Balyn offered to help him, the knight refused. "There's nothing you can do for me," he sobbed, as Balyn followed him through the forest foliage. "You might as well not bother. There's—"

At that moment, there was a quick scraping sound, and the sad knight lurched backwards and doubled over, screaming in pain. He fell writhing to the ground, and

Balyn saw blood spurting out of a hole in his breastplate, made by a sharp weapon.

"It's Sir Garlon!" choked the knight, his mouth swiftly filling with blood. "The knight who rides invisible! Get away from here at once, before he kills you!" he gulped, staring wildly at the shocked Balyn. "Quick, get away!"

These were his last words.

Balyn swiftly drew his terrible sword and waved it about, defending himself on all sides. There was silence.

Trembling, Balyn sheathed the sword and galloped away as fast as possible. Night was falling, and when he came to a small, friendly-looking castle, Balyn didn't hesitate to ask for a night's lodging. He was exhausted, and whatever he did, he couldn't seem to help anyone.

As he sat at a table laden with roast meats, delicious fresh bread, fruit and wine, Balyn made polite conversation with the lord of the castle, and his son, who was wrapped in bandages.

"Would you mind my asking how you came to be wounded?" Balyn enquired.

The injured son was about to speak, when his father interrupted. "That's Sir Garlon's work, the miserable coward! Edwin is lucky to be alive. If I could find a way to get revenge . . ."

"Sir Garlon?" said Balyn. "The invisible knight?"

"That's him," frowned the lord. "Oh, he's not invisible all the time, of course. Only when he feels like going out and attacking a few innocent bystanders for fun. In fact, he'll probably be at King Pelles's feast at Castle Carbonek tomorrow night. But I'd never be a match for him," the lord sighed, "even when he *is* visible. No one dares fight him ~ he's just too dangerous."

"I'll fight him for you," said Balyn, thinking of his powerful sword. "You've been very kind to me, and I'd be happy to challenge Sir Garlon. I assure you, I've nothing to lose," he added.

He was delighted that at last, he might be able to do some good by ridding these poor people of the evil Sir Garlon.

The following evening, Balyn's host showed him how to get to Pelles's castle, which lay in the wilderness, on the other side of the gnarled forest. "You haven't been invited, of course," said the lord, "but Pelles is a kind chap. He'll let you in. You'll see Sir Garlon. He's the one with the black helmet and the big black mustache."

Balyn soon reached the curious, ancient castle. He was immediately invited in to join the feast, and it didn't take him long to spot Sir Garlon.

He was one of the biggest, most frightening knights Balyn had ever seen. His dark, hooded eyes smoldered under his jet-black helmet, which he would not take off, even to eat his dinner. The shape of his wide, bushy mustache made him look as if he was smiling, but on closer inspection Balyn could see Sir Garlon's angry expression and cruel, twisted mouth.

Suddenly Sir Garlon pushed back his stool and stood up, banging the table and sending goblets and plates jangling to the ground.

"And what are *you* staring at?" he demanded viciously, glaring directly at Balyn. Everyone at the table froze.

But Balyn stayed calm. He felt for the leaf-engraved handle of the cursed sword hanging at his side, and as soon as he touched it, he was suffused with boldness and arrogance.

"At you, actually," he replied, in a rude, provocative tone of voice. "I just thought I'd have a good stare, while we've all got the chance."

"How dare you MOCK ME?!" roared Sir Garlon, flinging aside his stool and striding around the table to confront Balyn, who leaped up from his seat. As Garlon closed in, the cursed sword darted forward in Balyn's hand, gleaming in the candlelight. Then it suddenly slashed sideways, swiping off Sir Garlon's head in a single stroke.

The only noise to break the horrified silence was a heavy "thump", as the head, still wearing its heavy black helmet, landed on the wooden floor, its eyes bulging unpleasantly. Then the rest of Sir Garlon's body slowly toppled over and crashed onto the dinner table. The guests started screaming.

King Pelles, meanwhile, was marching furiously down the hall from the high table toward the scene.

"I don't know who you are," he yelled at Balyn, "but you were invited to join our feast in good faith!" He grabbed an iron mace, studded with spikes, that was hanging on the wall. "You've killed my friend and guest!" Pelles screeched hysterically. "Now get out of my castle this minute, before I kill

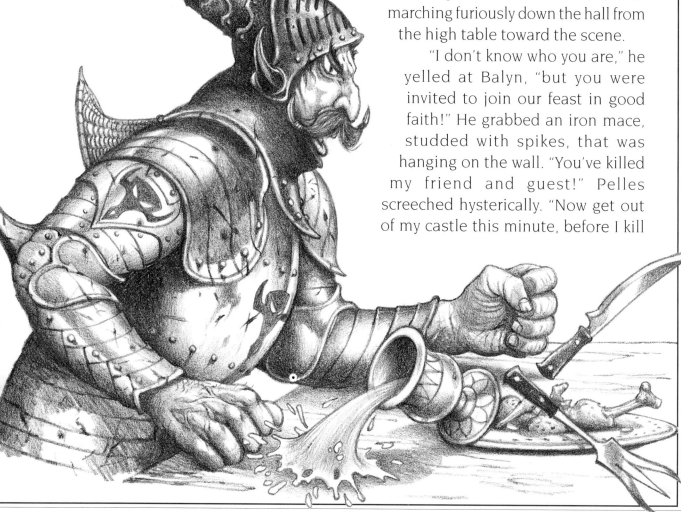

you!" And he started to chase Balyn down the hall.

The guests ducked and screamed as Balyn, waving his huge silver sword, and King Pelles, swinging his mace, tore through the banquet, weaving in and out of the tables, tripping on fallen goblets and slipping on spilled wine.

At last Balyn reached the end of the hall and desperately heaved open the heavy wooden door. He darted toward a staircase, the only exit he could see. Up and up into the darkness he ran, still grasping the sword which banged noisily on the stone steps, and along a musty-smelling corridor, with Pelles hurtling after him.

Suddenly Balyn saw a low, arched door and ducked through it. In front of him was another staircase winding away into the dank gloom. He leaped up the steps two at a time, grazing his knuckles on the narrow walls, as Pelles crashed through the doorway far below him.

Balyn reached the top of the narrow tower. He burst through a low door into a chamber filled with golden light.

He stopped and stared, his gasping breath echoing around the walls.

There, in front of him, was a table made of solid gold. Lying diagonally across it was a glittering silver spear. Its carved tip seemed to burn with a steady golden-green flame.

"TRAITOR!" screamed King Pelles, bursting through the little door and into the room, swinging the spiked mace violently around his head.

He lunged at Balyn, who wielded his cursed sword, trying to deflect the blow. But the force of the flying mace knocked the sword out of his hand, and it clattered uselessly to the floor.

Balyn backed away, pressing himself up against the golden table as Pelles stepped nearer, his face purple with fury, lifting up the mace for one final blow.

"P-please. . ." stammered Balyn, "I'm sorry, I never—"

But Pelles was about to strike. Balyn reached behind his back, scrabbling desperately for the strange silver spear he had seen. It was his last chance. As Pelles brought the mace down with a great roar of exertion, Balyn dodged aside and grabbed the spear from the table.

There was no time to think. He tightened his grip on the spear, and then swung it around and struck King Pelles as hard as he could.

The spear's blazing tip caught Pelles, who was still brandishing his mace above his head, on the side of the chest. Immediately his arms froze in mid-air, and a look of horror gripped his face. The mace slipped from his grasp, falling and jamming its spikes into the smooth wooden floorboards, and Pelles staggered backward, bleeding from a gaping wound in his side.

Balyn gazed, astonished. The spear seemed to be streaming with the brightest light he had ever seen, and he turned away, shielding his dazzled eyes. At that moment, there was an unbearably loud crash of thunder, and the golden room was plunged into darkness.

Balyn felt the building trembling

beneath him, and that was the last thing he remembered before the whole of Castle Carbonek began to crumble and split apart. Its towers and turrets collapsed, its walls and windows caved in, its roof tiles tumbled down, and all those who had been inside it ~ King Pelles, Sir Balyn, the banqueting guests, and the dead Sir Garlon ~ were buried under piles of rubble.

"Dear, dear," mumbled Merlin, shaking his head sadly. "Poor Balyn."

He had pulled the injured knight from the ruins of the castle. Only a small part of it remained standing, and there Merlin had installed the wounded King Pelles, along with the other surviving members of his household. There they would live, isolated in the wilderness, waiting for the visit of another Knight of the Round Table, many long years into the future.

Balyn started to wake up. The sorcerer magically soothed and healed his cuts and bruises, and placed the cursed sword once again in his hand.

"Where am I?" asked Balyn, dazed.

"You haven't got very far to go now," said Merlin kindly, leading the bewildered knight to his horse and helping him to climb into the saddle.

"Have courage, Sir Balyn. You must now seek your last adventure."

And, wiping a tear from his wrinkled old cheek, Merlin patted the horse, and watched as Balyn trotted away into the distance.

Balyn was standing in front of a white castle. He could hear the strained tooting of a hunting horn.

Then, suddenly, crowds of beautiful maidens started to stream out of the castle gates. There must have been a hundred of them, surrounding him, welcoming him, chattering and exclaiming and enticing him into the castle. Then dozens of knights appeared, followed by an elegant lady dressed all in white.

"Sir Balyn," said the lady, "you are welcome to stay in our castle and be our guest. But, just like everyone else who passes this way, you must fight with the Knight of the Island before you may continue your journey."

"Why?" asked Balyn. He didn't understand. Everything seemed fuzzy and uncertain, as if he was dreaming.

"Everyone who passes this way must fight the Knight of the Island," the lady repeated firmly.

"Who's he?" asked Balyn confusedly, as the knights and ladies began to lead his horse across the grass.

"You seem nervous," said a kind-looking knight at Balyn's side. "Here, you can borrow my shield. I can see that yours has been damaged."

Without thinking, Balyn accepted the new shield.

Then the knights and ladies took Balyn to a glass-calm lake. A small stone castle stood on an island near the shore, and its drawbridge was slowly being lowered, so that it formed a bridge to where Balyn and his horse were waiting.

. . .the whole of Castle Carbonek began to crumble and split apart.

Behind the drawbridge was a surprisingly small knight.

He and his horse were all dressed in red. He had a red shield, red tassels on his armor, and a red crest on his silver helmet.

"I am the Knight of the Island!" he cried, in a voice that sounded oddly familiar. "And all who pass this way must fight me!"

"I must accept whatever adventures fate hands out to me," Balyn said to himself quietly. Then he set his lance in position and spurred his horse forward across the bridge.

The two knights crashed together so hard that both their lances broke and they were thrown off their horses onto the grass. Balyn rolled over, grabbing for his sword, and as soon as he drew it out of the scabbard, he felt his strength returning. Filled with anger, he rushed at the Knight of the Island and they started dueling, swiping and stabbing fiercely at each other.

They fought until the sun began to go down and the grass was red with their blood, and still the Knight of the Island did not surrender. Balyn grew more and more vicious in his attacks.

At last both knights were so exhausted that they could fight no longer. The red knight sank to his knees, and Balyn fell back onto the bloody grass. When he looked up, the world seemed to be spinning around him. He could see the battlements of the white castle, lined with dozens of beautiful ladies, watching him, staring silently with their eyes wide open.

Now weak from loss of blood, Balyn crawled over to his adversary, and reached out a hand to him.

"Peace, Sir Knight," he groaned. "We have fought enough, and I fear we both have our death wounds."

He stopped to catch his breath, clutching at his side.

"But tell me," Balyn went on, "Knight of the Island, who are you? I've never before met a knight who could defeat me and my cursed sword."

By way of an answer, the other knight struggled with his helmet, loosened it and heaved it off.

"I am Sir Balan," he gasped, "a Knight of the Round Table."

Balyn stared in horror at his brother's face through the slits in his visor.

"Balan. . ." he whispered. "It's me ~ Balyn!" He too ripped off his helmet and the two men embraced in tears, although they were barely able to find the strength to lift their arms.

"What are you. . ? How did you. . ?" stuttered Balyn hopelessly. "What are you *doing* here? I thought you were on a brave and noble quest. . ."

"I was," Balan said through his tears, "but on my travels I wandered past this castle, and I had to fight the previous Knight of the Island. I managed to defeat him, and at first I was proud of my success. But I didn't realize it was a trick, set up by Morgan le Fay to entrap all Arthur's best knights. As the winner, my fate was to take the old knight's place, until someone strong enough to defeat me came along.

"Oh Balyn," Balan wailed, clutching his

head in his hands, "why didn't you wear your shield, and then I would have recognized you! How could I have let this happen?"

"It's not your fault," groaned Balyn. "It's me. After you left on your quest I. . . I was trying to prove myself to King Arthur, and I accepted a challenge to pull this sword out of a damsel's scabbard. But the sword was cursed, and ever since, it's. . . it's brought me nothing but bad luck."

Balan stared uncomprehendingly at his brother. They were both growing weaker every second.

"I killed the Lady of the Lake," Balyn sobbed, "and poor Sir Launceor, and Sir Garlon, and then ~ then ~ I don't know, it's all so confusing. . ."

Balyn looked painfully back at the shield he had borrowed, lying discarded on the bloodsoaked turf. If only he had kept his own shield ~ even though it was broken, it would have saved his life, which he could now feel ebbing away.

Then he looked at the cursed sword lying beside him, and suddenly remembered the warning words of the maiden he had taken it from:

"If you keep it, it will bring about your death. And with it, you'll kill your closest friend. . ."

With his last shred of energy, Balyn grabbed the sword and flung it as hard as he could away from him. It sailed a few feet through the air and landed heavily on the grass, not far away from where the two brothers, stained with each other's blood and tears, collapsed, limp and lifeless, into each other's arms.

Merlin was not far behind. He instructed the lady of the white castle to bury the two unfortunate brothers in one grave, with their sad story inscribed on their tombstone for all who passed by to read. He also made her promise to end the castle's gruesome tradition, and used his magic to crumble the drawbridge into the lake, so that there could be no more Knights of the Island.

Then he took Balyn's cursed sword, and buried it as deeply as he could.

Merlin was a wise, wonderful and clever sorcerer, who could change shape and read the minds of others, and even, sometimes, see into the future. But even his powerful magic had not been strong enough to undo the curse of the sword ~ even though he knew very well who had sent it, and why.

He cursed himself for teaching Morgan le Fay the ways of witchcraft and the secrets of sorcery, which she was now using to wreak havoc on the Kingdom of Logres. And Merlin knew that for her, this was no idle game. She had designs on the very throne itself, and he was sure she would have no qualms about doing whatever she had to do to weaken the Round Table and win what she wanted.

At that moment, the old magician resolved to do all he could to protect Arthur and his knights from Morgan's evil.

"For as long as I can, anyway," he murmured, picking up his great magic staff and wrapping his purple cloak around him, before disappearing in a tiny, floating wisp of smoke.

CHAPTER FIVE

THE TALE OF SIR LAUNFAL

"**S**ir Launfal," cooed Queen Guinevere seductively. "I *thought* I'd find you here."

"My lady!" exclaimed Sir Launfal, jumping up and bowing deeply as the queen sidled into the room. Guinevere had disturbed him at his work. He was busy writing the invitations to the midsummer feast, on pieces of purest parchment. But of course he had to be polite to the queen.

"Well, this is a pleasant surprise!" said Launfal. "May I be of assistance, your majesty?"

"Oh, Sir Launfal, there's no need to be so *formal*," giggled Guinevere. She came toward him and perched on the edge of the table. "I've just come for a little visit, of course!" She reached out and ran her fingertip down his nose. Launfal blushed.

"I thought perhaps we could go for a little walk together. Just you and me," added Guinevere, conspiratorially. "You must be exhausted, you've been working all *day*, my *poor* Sir Launfal," she clucked.

"Well, I . . ." Launfal began awkwardly. It would be very rude to reject the queen's offer, but he could hardly agree to see her behind King Arthur's back. He didn't want people to gossip.

"I don't really think that would be appropriate, your majesty," he tried to explain. "I can't ~ well, you see, I have a lot

of work to do, and. . ."

But it was already too late. Guinevere was offended. She stood up abruptly, arranging her skirt. "I see," she snapped.

"No. . . my lady, I didn't mean—" Sir Launfal stammered. "I do apologize, it's just that—"

"Goodbye," said the queen coldly, and strode out of the room.

Launfal sat down at his desk again, his head in his hands. What was he going to do? For weeks Guinevere had been batting her eyelashes at him and following him around. No one would dare mention it to Arthur, but his young wife did seem to have an unfortunate habit of taking a fancy to his knights. And at the moment, Sir Launfal seemed to be her favorite.

He couldn't think why. He was known for his kindness and generosity, but he was hardly the most handsome knight at Camelot, and he certainly wasn't the bravest. Why couldn't Guinevere find someone else to flirt with?

Sighing, he went back to his work.

Midsummer arrived, the feast was prepared, and knights, bishops, lords and ladies from all over the kingdom came, clutching their invitations. The best knights in the land jousted at the tournament, and, as usual, the bold Sir Lancelot was named the winner.

Then the celebrations began. The tables were heaped with food, musicians played late into the night, and the guests feasted, drank and danced. And the queen presented everyone in the room, as was the tradition, with a precious gift. Each lady received a gold necklace, and each gentleman a beautiful embroidered purse.

Except for Sir Launfal. The guests and the other knights watched, puzzled, as Guinevere deliberately passed him by on her tour of the great hall. He blushed again as everyone stared at him, wondering what he had done wrong.

Launfal could bear it no longer. Guinevere had been ignoring him for weeks, but this was the last straw. He would have to leave, before Arthur suspected something. He quietly slipped away to his living quarters high in one of Camelot's towers, gathered a few possessions into a bundle, and took his savings from under the bed. Then, while the revelers danced and sang and the musicians played, he mounted his horse and rode off into the night.

As dusk fell one winter evening, Guinevere climbed up the dusty stone steps to Sir Launfal's quarters, which now stood cold and empty. From downstairs, she could hear a faint, friendly clatter from the kitchen, where supper was being prepared.

She drifted over to the window and stared out at the evening gloom. She felt terribly guilty. Where was Sir Launfal? Would he ever come back? She had never meant to frighten him away.

At last the queen sighed a long, regretful sigh and went down to join her husband at the Round Table.

At that moment, Sir Launfal was riding dejectedly through a park, wondering what he was going to do. His horse was just about the only possession he had left. He hadn't been able to buy new clothes, and his old ones were ragged and dirty. He couldn't even afford a room for the night.

The trouble was, since he had left, poor Sir Launfal had been very unwise with his money. He had stayed as generous as ever, constantly giving away precious pieces of gold to traveling musicians, monks whose monasteries he stayed at, and beggars who couldn't believe their luck. Now he was in debt, and he was far too ashamed to go back to Camelot and confess that he was destitute.

Unfortunately, he was so busy thinking about his problems that he didn't look where he was going. His horse trotted right into a huge, swampy puddle, and started to slip and slide. The harness came loose, and all of a sudden Launfal found himself face down in the stinking mud.

As he picked himself up, he heard a crowd of locals laughing at him. Only the mud on his face hid his blushes as he stormed off into the forest, leaving his horse behind. He sank down under an old

. . . he mounted his horse and rode off into the night.

oak tree and wiped away a tear with his muddy hand. Perhaps ~ if he was lucky ~ some wild animal would come and eat him in the night, and that would be a convenient end to all his problems.

"Sir Launfal!"

"Wake up, gentle knight!"

Launfal didn't know whether he was awake or dreaming. It was dawn, and through the gloomy branches he thought he could see two breathtakingly lovely women coming toward him.

They wore shimmering gowns of silk, with green velvet cloaks over the top, embroidered with golden thread. On their heads were sparkling tiaras, decorated with dozens of precious jewels.

He *must* be dreaming.

"Sir Launfal," repeated one of the ladies. "You are to come with us."

"Our mistress Lady Tryamour *longs* for your presence," added the other, laughing sweetly. The women each took one of Launfal's hands, and led him, caked with mud as he was, through the trees. When they came within sight of a tall, striped pavilion, glowing with candlelight, they let go of Launfal's hands and gave him a gentle push.

"Go on," they whispered. "She's inside."

Launfal stepped apprehensively toward the richly decorated tent. Its walls were made of thick silk, its tentpoles were silver, and on the very top was an eagle made of solid gold, with glittering gems for eyes.

He gingerly pushed aside the silk curtain that was the pavilion's door.

"Come in," called a gentle female voice. Launfal stepped inside.

There, before him, surrounded by candles burning on golden candlesticks, was a bed with a purple silken cover. And under the cover, with her head sticking out, was another, even prettier lady, with soft golden hair. She smiled seductively at him.

"Oh! I . . . er, excuse me!" spluttered Sir Launfal, quickly stepping back outside the pavilion. "I had no idea you were. . . I beg your pardon, my lady!"

"Launfal," called the lady, with a sweet laugh like a running brook. "Come *back*. I want to talk to you."

So Launfal tiptoed back inside, and stood as far away from the bed as possible, turning his eyes away politely.

"Sir Launfal," said the lady, matter-of-factly. "Don't be so shy. I've brought you here to tell you something important."

Launfal looked up at her.

"The truth is," she went on, "I love you, Sir Launfal. I've been watching you, and I've decided you're the kindest, sweetest and most caring knight there is. So, I'm asking you to be *my* knight."

"My lady," breathed the astonished Launfal, staring at her. "Who are you?"

"I am the Lady Tryamour," the lady announced, proudly. "My father is the fairy king of the magical island of Olyroun." She slipped suddenly out from under her purple coverlet, and Launfal saw that she was wearing a demure blue dress, hemmed with glinting diamonds. She came over and took the knight's hand, looking longingly into his eyes.

"Say you'll be mine, Sir Launfal," she pleaded. "I'll reward you well."

"I will do as you command, of course," said Launfal. "But my lady, what could you possibly want with me? I'm not brave, I have no money, I'm estranged from King Arthur's court. And I'm covered in mud," he added. "In fact," he concluded sadly, "I'm just no good. You can't possibly want—"

"Launfal, Launfal," the lady whispered soothingly. "It's your *heart* I love. I've seen how generous you've been, how thoughtful you are. And as for money, that's easy enough to sort out. If you'll be my knight, I'll give you riches beyond your wildest dreams. I'll give you an enchanted purse that produces endless gold coins. I'll give you Blanchard, my magic horse, and my loyal squire, Gyfre, to serve you, and beautiful armor to wear when you go jousting, with my banner flying along behind you."

"But that's just it." Launfal hung his head awkwardly. He had known it couldn't work. "I'm useless at jousting."

"Not any more," smiled Lady Tryamour. "I'll make sure you don't get hurt. You'll have my magical powers on your side, remember?"

At last, Launfal began to relax. He could hardly believe what was happening to him, but he liked Lady Tryamour, and she obviously liked him. And whatever happened, his life couldn't possibly get any worse. "My Lady Tryamour," he announced finally, kneeling down before her. "I would be honored to be your knight."

Launfal stayed with Lady Tryamour for several days, feasting on delicate foods, taking romantic walks in the forest, and talking for hours on end. At last, however, the lady said she would have to go.

"Don't worry," she reassured him. "You can summon me at any time, simply by going somewhere alone and calling my name. But no one else must ever see me.

And I must warn you. . . " She looked into his eyes. "You must never, ever tell anyone about me. If you do, you'll lose everything."

Launfal promised that he wouldn't, and at that moment, Lady Tryamour, her beautiful pavilion and her lovely ladies-in-waiting disappeared into thin air.

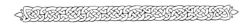

As the knight traipsed back through the forest, he began to wonder if he had imagined it all. A magical lady, offering to make him her knight and shower him with riches? He must have been hallucinating.

But just then, he saw a troop of ten men in impressive purple and gold uniforms. "Delivery for Sir Launfal!" one of them yelled.

"I'm here!" shouted Launfal, hurrying toward them excitedly.

Soon, Sir Launfal was sitting in the park in the morning sun, surrounded by his beautiful gifts from Lady Tryamour. He had new clothes and leather boots. He had a suit of the finest armor, a sword, a spear and a shield ~ and everything fitted him perfectly. He also had a small, embroidered purse, which seemed empty but each time he reached inside it, it produced a heavy gold coin.

And a few feet away, his new squire, Gyfre, tended to Blanchard, his magnificent new white horse.

The first thing Launfal did was pay off his debts. Then he bought a large house and employed lots of servants, all of whom he paid very well, and returned to his old generous ways.

He paid for prisoners to be released from jail. He funded monasteries and hospitals, and always tipped musicians in the street. He held feasts for poor people and beggars. And every night, alone in his room, he called for his Lady Tryamour, who came and lived with him like a wife, except that no one ever knew about her.

Eventually, word of Sir Launfal's riches and generosity got back to Camelot, and one morning, a messenger galloped up to his house with an invitation:

The noble knight and famed gentleman
Sir Launfal
is hereby graciously invited to
King Arthur's Midsummer Feast
at the Castle of Camelot

On the back was scrawled: *"Please come. Your old friends, Arthur and Guinevere."*

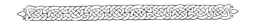

Camelot towered above Sir Launfal as he approached on Blanchard, in his new armor, with Gyfre following behind. The trumpets rang out, the sun glittered on the roof tiles, and the flags flapped in the breeze.

"Launfal! It's good to see you!" called Sir Gawain from the battlements.

"Look at his finery!" gasped the ladies as Launfal trotted on under the battlements. "He's so handsome in that armor!"

"So," said Arthur kindly, after he had embraced his friend, "you must have run into some good luck! Tell us how you came by such riches."

"Well, it was nothing to do with me,

really," began Launfal modestly. "My lady—"

Just in time, he remembered that he must not breathe a word about Lady Tryamour.

"My lady the queen is looking most enchanting today," he corrected himself. Guinevere blushed and smiled coyly at him.

But soon the pleasantries were over, and it was time for the tournament to begin. Launfal was to joust first, against Sir Percival. It was years since he'd taken part in a tournament, but now he had a lady, he must fight in her name.

The two knights faced each other across the field, shields raised and lances set in position. At a trumpet blast from the battlements, they spurred their horses and galloped toward each other, each aiming his lance at the other's breastplate.

Through the narrow slit in his visor, Launfal saw Percival, dressed from head to toe in shimmering silver armor, thundering toward him. He gripped his lance even tighter and, at the moment of impact, planted its blunt tip in the middle of Percival's stomach, while deflecting Percival's lance with his shield. A huge cheer went up as Percival flew off his horse and landed with a clattering thump on the grass, and Launfal rode triumphantly past, toward the royal box where he dismounted and bowed deeply before the queen. Then he went and helped Sir Percival up, and shook hands with him.

"First game to Sir Launfal!" shouted the scorekeeper.

Late that afternoon, Sir Launfal was still jousting. He had beaten or matched everyone he had fought, and even more surprisingly, he had enjoyed himself. He began to see why all the other knights loved jousting so much: the tension as the two competitors came face-to-face, the excitement as they clashed together, the cheering and shouting, the gossip about who would win the tournament. And the best part was that he was with his old friends. Launfal sighed with satisfaction as he gazed around the jousting field.

And that was when, out of the corner of his eye, he saw an absolutely vast knight, on a *huge* horse, weaving his way through the crowd. His shield bore the sign of a hawk, and his armor was studded with vicious spikes. Launfal was sure he hadn't seen him before. He went over to Arthur.

"Who's that?" he asked, pointing.

"Looks like trouble," said Sir Gawain.

"I'd better find out," murmured Arthur, grabbing his crown and striding out onto the field. The strange knight galloped up to him and reared his horse frighteningly, forcing Arthur to take a step back.

"Welcome to Camelot! I am King Arthur," announced the king in his most official voice. "And I don't believe that you, Sir, were on our guest list. Would you be so kind as to tell us your name?"

"SIR VALENTINE OF LOMBARDY," boomed the knight, in a voice so deep it made the flagpoles tremble, "IS MY NAME."

"And have you come to take part in our tournament, Sir Valentine?"

"INDEED," roared the giant stranger. "I COME TO FIGHT THE BEST KNIGHT ON THE FIELD!"

"Well," said Arthur, glancing round awkwardly. "Normally, of course, that would be Sir Lancelot." He saw Lancelot shaking his head and trying to sink down in his chair. "But today, we have another knight leading the field. Sir Launfal, would you. . . ?"

Sir Launfal felt the blood draining from his face. He felt sick. He managed a weak smile for the crowd, but he could hardly stop himself from trembling as he went to remount Blanchard.

"Go on, Launfal!" yelled the crowd. "You can do it!"

"You'll be fine," murmured Gyfre as he handed Launfal his shield, flipped his visor down and patted Blanchard affectionately. "Remember, aim for the body."

Soon, Sir Launfal and Sir Valentine faced each other on the field, lances in position. The crowd screamed itself into a frenzy, the trumpet sounded, and Blanchard bolted forward.

Launfal concentrated hard as he pounded toward the huge knight. At the last second, he pointed his lance upward so as to hit Sir Valentine's torso, and caught him squarely in the middle of the chest.

But Launfal had been aiming so carefully that he had forgotten to use his shield. Something large, hard and heavy whacked him in the stomach, making him gasp for breath. It was Valentine's lance. Both knights flew through the air and landed in crumpled heaps on the ground.

"A draw!" shouted the scorekeeper, who had scrawled the name "Sir Valentine" in chalk at the bottom of his scoreboard.

Sir Launfal picked himself up, examined the dent in his armor, adjusted his helmet, and set off to bow before the queen as usual.

But Sir Valentine had other ideas. He stumbled onto his extremely large feet, and lurched toward Sir Launfal, drawing an enormous sword as he did so.

"Game over!" the scorekeeper yelled anxiously. "All done! Time for tea!"

"TO THE DEATH!" boomed Sir Valentine, brandishing his sword at Launfal.

"Wait!" It was Gyfre. He was running onto the field, dragging Sir Launfal's sword behind him. He placed it firmly in the knight's hand, and backed away.

"How did I get here?" thought Launfal miserably to himself, as he circled cautiously around Sir Valentine. "He'll make mincemeat of me."

At that moment Sir Valentine decided to strike. He swung his sword around and whacked Launfal on the side of the head. Launfal's helmet protected him, but he was knocked sideways. Furiously, he rushed back at the giant knight, who was laughing complacently, and thrust his sword into Valentine's side. The crowd went wild.

"WORM!" screamed Sir Valentine, apoplectic with rage. "DOG MEAT! CONSIDER YOURSELF A DEAD MAN!" And he lifted his sword in both of his mighty hands, and brought it slashing down through the air. Launfal dodged to the right just in time to avoid being sliced in two. Valentine's sword plowed into the grass, where it stuck, and as he tried to haul it out, Launfal kicked his enemy's hands away from the hilt. Slashing and jabbing with his sword, he chased Sir Valentine away from his own weapon. The crowd roared with laughter. Finally he managed to leap

forward and grab Sir Valentine by the ankles, and the vast, towering figure came crashing down onto the turf. Launfal leaped on top of him and pointed his sword at his throat.

"Game over!" called the scorekeeper again. "Game to Sir Launfal!"

There was no more fighting that day. After Sir Valentine had been released, he left, shamefaced, for Lombardy, vowing never to mess with King Arthur's knights again. Sir Launfal was awarded the grand prize, and made guest of honour at the feast.

As midsummer's day turned to midsummer's night, the musicians arrived and the party began. All the ladies wanted to dance with Sir Launfal, as he took his turn on the green lawns of Camelot in the warm night air. But although out of politeness he danced with every one of them, all he could think of was his Lady Tryamour, and how grateful he was to her. He only wished she could be with him. How they would dance! Everyone would be amazed by her beauty and grace.

"Dreaming the night away, are we, Sir Launfal?" Launfal looked around and saw Guinevere beside him.

"You were so *manly* today," the queen said admiringly, in a low voice. "So *hand*some. You know I always did find you attractive." She gave him a coy glance. "Are you *sure* you haven't changed your mind? You remember our little agreement." She sidled closer to him. "Kiss me, Sir Launfal," she purred.

"Madam," coughed Launfal, shifting away. "We had no agreement. You know very well I could not be a traitor to my king."

Guinevere's face grew sour. "Have it your own way!" she grumbled. "But I must say, I don't know what's wrong with you. You don't seem to be interested in anyone!"

Suddenly Launfal lost his temper. He couldn't stop himself.

"I'll have you know, your *majesty*," he snarled, "that I have a lady of my own, and what's more, she's a lot more beautiful than you are!" Guinevere stared at him in shock.

"In fact," Launfal went on, "her ugliest, most useless maid would make a better queen than you!" And he stomped away.

Suddenly he stopped. He remembered his lady's warning. And as he did so, his fine clothes started to disappear. Within seconds, he was standing there, surrounded by richly dressed lords and ladies, wearing nothing but his old rags. He felt in his pockets. His embroidered purse was gone.

Launfal desperately began looking for somewhere to hide. He found a small closet and ducked into it. "Lady Tryamour," he called desperately. "My lady," he sobbed, "I'm sorry. I'm sorry! Please come back!"

Silence. A moth flapped out of the gloom and brushed against his face.

Then he heard angry voices. "Where is Sir Launfal?" someone shouted. The cupboard door was opened, and there stood King Arthur, frowning furiously. "What's this I hear about you insulting my wife?!" he demanded. "How dare you ask her to kiss you! And what on earth are you wearing? Arrest him!"

"I didn't, I swear," said Sir Launfal helplessly as he stood before Arthur in the hall, flanked by guards. "I never asked her

to kiss me." But he couldn't tell the king that it had been Guinevere who had asked *him*, that she had lied to Arthur. "I did say. . ."

"Yes?"

"I did say that my lady's ugliest maid would make a better queen than her," confessed Launfal. "And I'm very sorry."

"What lady is this?" Arthur wanted to know. "I didn't know you had a lady."

"The most beautiful lady in the world," Launfal began, wistfully. "The loveliest, the kindest. . ." His voice trailed off. Would he ever see her again?

"Well," said Arthur, who liked Launfal and didn't really want to punish him, "I'll give you a chance. Bring your lady to Camelot, and if she really is the most beautiful lady in the world ~ more beautiful than the queen, even," he added, "then I'll let you off. You've got two weeks. Otherwise. . ."

Arthur couldn't bring himself to say it. But he and Launfal both knew that the official punishment for insulting the queen was death.

For those two weeks poor Sir Launfal tried everything he could think of to win his lady back. His house and servants were gone, and so were Blanchard and Gyfre. He had to wander the streets, begging for food. He called for Lady Tryamour, praying that she would come, but she never did. He thought of his brief glory at the tournament ~ but without a horse, how could he prove his bravery? He went to the spot where they had met, and waited all night, kneeling on the wet grass. Nothing happened.

"Well?" said King Arthur, on the fourteenth day, when Launfal turned up alone at Camelot to meet his fate. "Where is she?" Arthur was starting to get anxious. He had been sure that Launfal would have no problem bringing his lady to the castle.

In front of the king, the queen, and all the knights, Sir Launfal tried to explain. He told them how he had been poor and destitute, and had met the strange lady in the forest, and how she had given him riches in return for being her knight, and how they had been as in love and as happy as ever knight and lady were. But he had broken his promise, and boasted about her, and now she was gone.

"I can't go back on my word," said Arthur sadly. "You know what the official punishment is."

Guinevere looked guilt-stricken. She had never meant Launfal to die. And none of the knights, who remembered Launfal's kindness in the past, could bear to see him hanged.

"I propose that Sir Launfal be exiled, instead of executed," said Sir Gawain quickly.

"Seconded!" yelled another knight from the back of the hall.

"Wait a minute," said Arthur. "I'll have to go and look that up in the rulebook."

Just then, ten beautiful ladies on white horses rode in. "Thank goodness!" grinned Gawain, helping the ladies dismount. "She's one of these, isn't she? She must be!"

"No," said Launfal sadly. But then he noticed something. The ladies looked familiar. He was sure he'd seen their sparkling tiaras somewhere before.

"One of those, then?" asked Sir Gawain, standing in the doorway. He had spotted ten more maidens galloping toward Camelot across the meadow.

"I'm afraid not," said Sir Launfal,

agitatedly. He almost wished they would get it over with and hang him.

"Now then," mumbled Arthur, turning the dusty pages. "It says here, hanging may be transmuted to exile if, and only if—"

"Royal King Arthur!" announced one of the maidens. "Make way for the arrival of our lady!" The twenty women, in their white silk dresses and green cloaks, lined up to form a human corridor leading toward the throne where Arthur sat, with the ragged Launfal before him.

Launfal looked up.

He couldn't believe his eyes.

There, at the other end of the corridor, stood a familiar, stunningly beautiful figure. She was smiling warmly at him.

"My lady. . ." breathed Launfal in a whisper. "I thought you would never come! I let you down. . . I broke my promise. . ."

"You were the perfect knight," Lady Tryamour corrected him. "You may have broken your promise. But at the tournament you proved your courage, your virtue and your loyalty to your lady. One small mistake in your manners," she said, looking slightly disdainfully at Guinevere, who bowed her head, "is understandable."

Sir Launfal and his beautiful lady were married that day, and Launfal agreed to return to the Round Table. From that day on, the happy couple shared his chambers high up in the towers of Camelot. And Guinevere never intruded on Sir Launfal again.

In fact, she had now decided she liked a different knight altogether. But that's another story.

CHAPTER SIX

SIR GAWAIN AND THE GREEN KNIGHT

"**S**ilence!" shouted Sir Gawain one New Year's Day, banging his goblet on the Round Table. The whole court had gathered in the great hall at Camelot, and the first course of a huge feast had just been carried in to the sound of a trumpet fanfare.

"Silence for the king!" yelled Gawain again. The music faded, the babble of voices died down and soon only the crackling of the log fires broke the silence.

"Thank you, ladies and gentlemen," said Arthur. "Now, before we begin this splendid feast, what spectacle or adventure awaits us?"

It was a custom at Camelot that on feast days the king would not start eating until he had seen a brave deed or a strange marvel, or heard a tale of a dangerous quest.

"Come on, Knights of the Round—"

A loud commotion out in the courtyard and the clatter of horseshoes on stone cut him off in mid sentence. The massive doors of the hall flew open, and in rode an enormous man on an enormous horse.

He was far taller than any ordinary man, with huge hands, large, powerful limbs and piercing red eyes set in a fierce face. But the most extraordinary thing about him, which made everyone gape in amazement, was that he was bright green all over!

Not only were his clothes green, but his hands were green and his face was green. His long, thick hair and the big, shaggy beard that spread all over his chest were as green as grass. Even his gigantic horse was green from head to hoof. He carried no weapons except a colossal green battleax clasped in one hand. The other hand held a big branch of holly high above his head.

The Green Knight rode proudly through the stunned silence of the hall, surveying the scene. Then he cast the holly down on the floor and called out: "Who's in charge here?" His big, booming voice echoed around the cavernous hall.

No one answered. Like everyone else, Arthur was dumbstruck. He stared at the bright green figure in total astonishment. Several moments elapsed before he had recovered enough to greet the stranger and invite him to the feast.

"I haven't come to eat with you," said the Green Knight bluntly, "and don't worry, I'm not here for a fight, either. That's why I brought a branch instead of a sword ~ and if I wanted a fight, I'd be wearing my armor, wouldn't I?" Arthur breathed a quiet sigh of relief; the prospect of having to get up to fight this huge man instead of sitting down for a feast was not one he relished.

"What I *can* offer you," the knight went

. . . in rode an enormous man on an enormous horse.

on, swinging his ax casually, "is a little New Year's challenge. The fame of your knights has spread, you see. We've even heard about their brave deeds in my castle in the north, so I've come to offer them a small test to find out if their reputation is deserved."

"Sir," replied the king, "I'm sure there are plenty of people here who would joust with you, or fight in single combat, if that's what you have in mind."

"No!" boomed the knight. "I've told you, I don't want to fight. These boys would have no chance against me, anyway. They're far too feeble." He was staring directly at Gawain. A wave of anger swept around the table, but nobody dared to respond.

"But if anyone here is brave enough to exchange just one blow for another," he said, "I'll hand over my ax and let him strike me first. He can aim the blow wherever he wants, and I promise I won't even flinch, as long as I can return the blow exactly a year from today."

At this point, the Green Knight rolled his red eyes ferociously, brandished his ax and looked all around the hall for someone to answer his challenge. When nobody stepped forward, he roared with laughter.

"Is this really the great court of King Arthur?" roared the knight scornfully. "And can these really be the famous Knights of the Round Table? I don't know how you earned your reputation, when just the mention of an ax makes you all tremble with fear!" Then he rocked with laughter again, until Arthur's face went red with embarrassment. But his shame soon turned into anger, and

unable to bear the gibes a moment longer, he sprang forward.

"This is madness, Sir!" he said, striding over to face the huge man. "But if you really want to play such a stupid game, give me your ax and get ready!" The Green Knight dismounted and handed the heavy weapon to Arthur. The king gripped its huge handle firmly, and was preparing to strike when Sir Gawain jumped up from his seat.

"Please, Uncle," he said, "let me accept instead of you. I've yet to prove myself worthy as a Knight of the Round Table, and this could be my chance."

Arthur was reluctant to let Gawain take his place, but he was swayed by the eager expression on the young man's face, so he handed him the ax and wished him luck.

"I'm glad that at least one of you so-called knights is brave enough to accept," said the Green Knight. "What's your name, boy?"

"My name is Gawain," came the answer, "and I'm a Knight of the Round Table, not a boy. And as a knight I give you my promise that I will strike one blow, on the understanding that whatever happens, you will return the blow a year from today."

"I'm pleased you accept the terms of the agreement," said the knight. "After you've struck your blow, I'll tell you who I am and how to find me in a year's time. But now, let's see what you can do with the ax."

The knight then kneeled down on the floor, bowed his head and pulled his long hair forward to expose the back of his green neck. Gawain gripped the ax, took a deep breath, and with all his strength swung it high into the air. Then, taking a small step forward, he brought it swiftly down on the knight's bare neck with such great force that the razor sharp blade sliced straight through the flesh and bone, and sent sparks flying as it hit the cold stone floor.

The huge head thudded to the ground and rolled across the floor. Blood spurted from the severed neck, bright red against the green, but the knight did not falter or fall. He stood up and strode forward, grabbed his head by the hair and, turning to his horse, swung himself into the saddle as if nothing unusual had happened!

Amidst gasps of astonishment, he raised his head in his hand and turned its face toward Gawain. Out of the mouth came these words:

"Keep your promise, Sir Gawain,
To meet me next New Year's Day.
It will not be hard to track me down,
Though my castle is far away.

Through the mountains and valleys of Wales,
To the Forest of Wirral beyond,
At the place called the Green Chapel,
There we will seal our bond.

Ask for the knight of that chapel,
For many there know me by name.
If you search me out, you shall find me.
If you fail, you shall live in shame."

And with that, the Knight of the Green Chapel spurred his horse to a gallop and clattered out of the doors, across the courtyard and away into the night through the swirling snow, still dangling his head by its long, green hair.

The year passed quickly for Gawain, as season followed season. The New Year celebrations came to an end, the snow melted and fresh green leaves appeared on the trees. The chill winds of spring gave way to summer's heat, and the sweet, rich scent of roses faded all too quickly when the meadows were filled with the cries of reapers. At last, when the harvest had been gathered in and the woodpiles were stacked high, Gawain began to prepare for his quest to meet the Green Knight.

On the first morning of November, he strapped on his armor and sword, and with the Green Knight's ax in his hand, mounted his horse, Gringalet. His squire handed him his helmet. Then, remembering the knight's words, Gawain set off on his mysterious quest, riding alone through the Kingdom of Logres to the wild mountains and deep wooded valleys of Wales ~ through driving rain and snow, across icy rivers shrouded in fog, through deep, dark forests and along lonely, windswept clifftops.

At night he slept in his armor among the cold, craggy rocks, fearful of attack from wolves, bears and robbers. By day he pressed onwards, fighting long and bloody battles with the dragons, monsters and

. . .fighting long and bloody battles with dragons. . .

giants which in those days still lived in the wilderness. Few others could have survived all the dangers and hardships of that bitter winter, but Gawain struggled on until he reached the Forest of Wirral. He asked everyone he met if they knew the Knight of the Green Chapel, but no one had even heard of him.

On Christmas Eve, cold, weary and disheartened, Gawain prayed he might find somewhere to shelter. All of a sudden, the swirling mists parted, the marshland gave way to parkland, and in the distance he caught sight of a magnificent castle.

"Thank God," thought Gawain. "Now I can only pray that whoever lives there will welcome me in for Christmas."

His prayers were soon answered, for he was met with a warm welcome when he knocked on the gate. The moment

he entered the yard, servants and squires scurried round to help him dismount. Gringalet was led away to the stables, and the grateful Gawain was shown to a hall where a big log fire burned in the hearth.

The lord of the castle, a large, genial man with a red beard and thick, red hair, clasped Gawain firmly by the hand, welcomed him to his home and invited him to stay for as long as he wished. He said that everyone was delighted that a famous Knight of the Round Table had found his way to such a remote castle.

Gawain was treated with utmost hospitality. The squires took him to a chamber, helped him take off his rusty armor and gave him warm, fur-lined robes to wear. Then they led him back to a comfortable chair near the fire, where a sumptuous feast awaited him.

After the meal, the lady of the castle came in. She was one of the most beautiful women Gawain had ever seen in his life. Gawain spoke to her very politely, bowing deeply and kissing her hand,

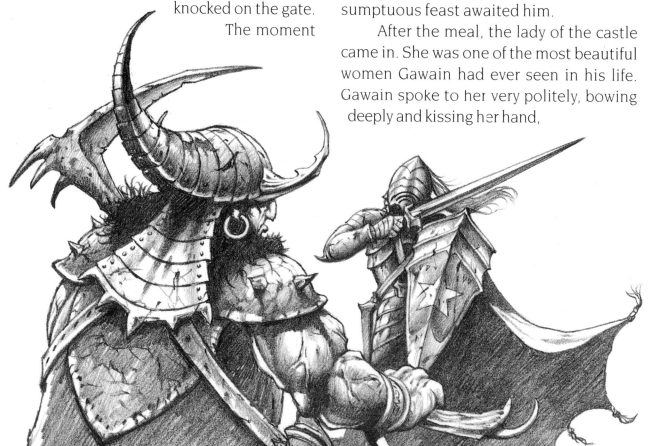

smiling, laughing and taking every opportunity to display the skills in conversation and courtly manners for which he was justly renowned.

On Christmas Day, many more guests arrived, and three whole days passed quickly in feasting and celebration. Gawain enjoyed himself so much that he almost forgot why he was there. At each meal he found the lady sitting next to him, always chattering, giggling and ordering her servants to attend to him.

On the fourth day, most of the guests left early. But when Gawain began to get ready to go, the lord stopped him.

"Must you leave us so soon?" he asked. "Please stay a little longer, unless you think we're unworthy to have such a noble guest."

"It's certainly not that," said Gawain. "You've been extremely generous, but I must leave to find the Green Chapel. I made a promise that I'd be there on New Year's Day, and I don't even know where it is yet."

"Then we're all in luck!" said the lord. "The Green Chapel is only a few miles from here, so you can stay with us until the day of your appointment. We'd be delighted to have you." Gawain was relieved to hear this, and tried to put all thoughts of the Green Knight out of his mind as he agreed to stay.

"I'm sure you're still tired from your journey," said the lord. "What you need is rest and plenty to eat before you go. Why don't you sleep in tomorrow and come down when you feel like it? I'm going to be out in the forest all day, hunting deer, but my wife can look after you." Gawain said he thought this was a good idea.

"And let's make a bargain," added the lord, "that in the evening we'll trade whatever we've won during the day."

Gawain agreed to play this game, even though he didn't really know what the lord meant.

The next morning, when the lord left, Gawain dozed in his bed, protected from drafts by the thick curtains which hung all around it. He was awakened by a soft tapping on the door, and peeping out from behind the curtains, he saw the lady of the castle poking her head into the room.

"Good morning, Sir Gawain," she said sweetly. "It's time to wake up. It would be a shame to spend the morning in bed, when we've so much to talk about." Then she closed the door gently. Gawain was still sleepy and didn't feel like leaving his warm bed. But he didn't want to be rude, so he got up, dressed and went downstairs.

"Here's my favorite knight, at last!" giggled the lady when she saw him. "And as my husband's away, I can do exactly what I want with you!" She straightened his tunic and brushed imaginary specks from his shoulders. Then she sat down at the table and patted the space next to her. "Now come and sit beside me and we'll have a little chat."

And so she went on, talking, laughing and flirting all morning. Gawain responded courteously but coolly, pretending that he didn't understand what she was hinting at. Although she was so beautiful, he knew she was his host's wife, and that he was a Knight of the Round Table. In fact, he was not really in the mood for games, as the shadow of the Green Knight loomed ever closer.

When the lady finally got up to go, Gawain didn't stop her, so she said: "It's hard to believe that you're really Sir Gawain."

"And why's that?" he asked anxiously, worried that he had offended her.

"Because Sir Gawain would never spend such a long time with a lady and then let her leave without asking for a kiss."

"If that is your wish, I will comply," he replied. She leaned forward gracefully and kissed him, then got up and left.

When the lord came home with the deer he had killed that day, he offered them to Gawain in exchange for whatever he had won. In return, Gawain put his hands around the lord's neck and kissed him.

"Is that what you won today?" asked the lord, rather surprised.

"That's all," said Gawain, "and I give it to you freely, just as it was given to me."

"But where did you get it from?" asked the lord.

"Telling you that was not part of our agreement," said Gawain, and they both laughed. On the way to supper they agreed to play the same game the following day.

The next morning, the lord left early to hunt wild boar in the marshes. After he'd left, the lady spent all morning trying to seduce Gawain. But once again he resisted her advances by turning them into a joke, though with such skill that he managed not to offend her. By the end of the morning, all that she had given him were two kisses.

When the lord returned, he presented Gawain with a huge wild boar, and without explanation, Gawain gave him two kisses.

"You have done well!" said the lord, as they went to supper.

All evening the lady flirted with Gawain, right under her husband's nose, and all evening Gawain treated her very politely. At last, the lord announced that the next day he was going to hunt foxes, and suggested that they should renew their bargain. Gawain agreed. The next morning, when the lord left at sunrise, he lay in bed, having nightmares about the Green Knight.

He was awakened by sunshine streaming into the room as the lady threw open the window to let in the frosty morning air.

"Still asleep, Sir Gawain?" she asked. "And on such a fine morning. What a lazy knight you are today!" When he came down, she kissed him good morning. She looked astonishingly beautiful in her long robe and green sash, her lustrous hair decorated with sparkling jewels. They chatted all morning, and she flirted even more than usual. Gawain trod a perilous path ~ if he rejected her, he might offend her, yet if he responded in the way she wanted, he'd be betraying his host. So, cleverly, he kept avoiding the subject, and tactfully fended off her declarations of love.

"Your heart must be made of ice," she said at last. "Why do I only get one kiss? You must have another lady at Camelot."

"No other lady has my love, but I cannot love you, even though you are so lovely," he replied, "for you already have a husband who's a better man than me."

"But just for today we could forget that, couldn't we?" she asked.

"I'm afraid not," he replied. "Because I am a knight, and I would bring shame upon my knighthood if I forgot that even for a moment."

"You may be a virtuous knight, but I'll have to spend the rest of my life in mourning," she said, sighing and kissing him sweetly. "But if you'll accept nothing else, please at least take this sash." She unfastened the green silk sash and offered it to Gawain, but he refused to take it.

"You're wrong if you think it's not worth much," she said, still holding out the sash. "It has magical powers. Anybody who wears it cannot be killed."

Gawain needed no more persuading. He was thinking again about the Green Knight. Something that might save his life was impossible to resist. He took the sash.

"Don't worry," said the lady, "my husband needn't know about it.

Hide it under your clothes and don't tell him." With this, she kissed him for a third time and left.

That evening, when Gawain met the lord, he said straight away: "Let me be the first to give you my winnings," and kissed him three times. He didn't mention the sash.

"You've done even better than yesterday," said the lord, "and all I have to offer is a smelly fox skin!"

After dinner, Gawain thanked his host and reminded him of his appointment at the Green Chapel. The lord promised to provide a guide to show him the way.

Gawain hardly slept a wink that night. He got up before it was light and put on his newly polished armor, not forgetting first to tie the sash around his waist. Then he seized his weapons, went out to the stables, mounted Gringalet and followed his guide out of the gates.

It was a bitterly cold day. Snow had piled up in great drifts overnight and the freezing wind chilled the two men to the bone. They rode through driving sleet across a valley and up a wooded hillside onto high moorland cloaked in fog. At last the guide stopped and turned to Gawain.

"We're not far from the chapel now, Sir," he said. "I'm turning back, and if I were you I'd do the same. That knight's an evil monster. He'll kill anyone who goes near him. Why don't you go home now? ~ I promise I won't tell anybody. I beg you not to go down there, Sir. . . you won't escape."

"I thank you for your advice," said Gawain to the terrified man, "but I am a knight and I must keep my promise. It would be cowardly to run away now." He tried to sound calm, but couldn't stop his armor rattling as he trembled with fear.

"Well, if you're so eager to die, I'm not going to stop you," said the guide. "Follow this path to the bottom of the valley. When you come to a clearing, you'll see the chapel on your left. Now goodbye and good luck. You'll need it. I wouldn't be in your shoes for all the gold in the world!" Then he galloped away, as though fleeing the devil himself.

Gawain's heart was thumping wildly as he spurred Gringalet on down a winding path and into the gloomy valley. By the time he reached the clearing he was numb with fear. On his left there was nothing that resembled a chapel, only a mound near a waterfall. He rode over, dismounted and began to walk around. Could this grass-covered hill be what he was looking for? It had several openings, and was hollow. He plucked up enough courage to poke his head inside. It was dark, dank, and empty.

"What a strange place," he thought, as he climbed onto the top of the mound.

Just then he was startled by a loud grinding noise which echoed all around the valley. It sounded like a reaper sharpening his scythe. With horror, Gawain realized it was the sound of an ax being sharpened.

"Where are you?" he yelled. There was no reply. The grinding continued.

"Show yourself, Green Knight. Let's get this over with."

"Wait!" boomed a voice from above. "You'll get what you've been promised, just as soon as my weapon is sharp."

Then, suddenly, out of a hole in the grassy mound, appeared the Green Knight, effortlessly whirling a massive new ax above his head, which was once more firmly attached to his body. He looked even larger and fiercer than

64

Gawain remembered.

"Welcome to my humble abode, Sir Gawain," he said. "You've arrived in good time to keep our appointment. Well, don't worry, you'll soon be repaid for your efforts. Now, off with that helmet and take what you're owed. Offer no more resistance than I did when you sliced off my head with one blow."

"Get ready to strike," said Gawain. "I'll do nothing to stop you." He knelt on the snow-covered grass, bowed his head and bared his neck, muttering a prayer under his breath. The Green Knight whirled the ax around, then raised it above his head and was just about to strike when Gawain twitched.

"The brave Sir Gawain isn't afraid of the sound of an ax, is he?" taunted the knight. "I didn't flinch before you cut off my head."

"It happened once," said Gawain, "but it won't happen again, even though I cannot replace my head, as you can. Strike away."

Once more the Green Knight whirled his ax and got ready to strike. Gawain shut his eyes, clenched his teeth and held his breath. The knight raised the ax high into the air and brought it down, missing Gawain's head by a hair's breadth, but this time Gawain didn't move a muscle, even as he heard the blade whistle past his ear.

"That's more like it!" said the Green Knight. "Your courage has returned. Now pull your hood back a bit, so I can make a nice clean cut."

"Just get on with it!" screamed Gawain suddenly. "Stop playing games. Are you afraid to kill me?"

The Green Knight swung the weapon a third time, and, with a mighty groan, brought the blade hurtling to the ground.

Gawain took a deep breath and opened his eyes. He was still alive! Then he felt a stinging pain on the side of his neck. His fingers reached up and found a thin gash where the ax had nicked his flesh. Blood dripped onto the snow. He sprang up, seized his sword and in an instant was ready to fight.

"No more!" he said. "You've had your chance. I've kept my side of the bargain, now if you try to strike me again, I'll hit back, harder than you could ever imagine."

The Green Knight stepped back and leaned on his ax. He watched Gawain calmly for a while and then said quietly:

"I will not strike again, Sir Gawain. You're released from your bond. I could have cut off your head, but I had already tested you and found you to be true. The first blow and the second were for the one and two kisses from my wife that you gave back to me at my castle. Don't look so surprised, Sir Gawain ~ I know about what went on between you, because I put her up to it. Only the third time did you fail, when you gave me the kisses but not the sash that you have hidden under your armor, and for that small failing I gave you this small wound.

"You have proved to be a noble and honest knight. If you had yielded to temptation and brought shame on your knighthood, your head would be rolling around at my feet, but your only fault was love of your own life ~ I know that's why you took the sash ~ and for that I forgive you."

"Take the wretched thing!" said Gawain, pulling out the sash from under his armor. "I was a coward to accept it and a fool not to tell you about it. I've broken my promise and am not worthy to be called a knight. Kill me now. I deserve to die."

"Don't be so hard on yourself for such a small mistake," said the knight, with a laugh that Gawain knew well. "You've suffered enough. Now keep the sash and come back to my castle to celebrate."

"This time I must refuse," said Gawain, "but I'll keep the sash as a reminder of my weakness. Now I must go home, but before I do, tell me who you are. Where do you get your powers from? How can you turn into a green man who can survive having his head cut off?"

"My name is Sir Bercilak," the knight replied, "and it was Morgan le Fay who devised this plan. She came to my castle one day and cast a spell to turn me into the Green Knight. Then she sent me to Camelot. She also hatched the plot to see if you could resist my wife's charms. She wanted to see if Arthur's knights really deserved their reputation for chivalry and bravery, and you, Sir Gawain, have proved beyond all doubt that they do."

For a moment, Gawain wondered why Morgan le Fay would do this; but he thanked Sir Bercilak

anyway for his kind words, said goodbye and set off. With his ordeal finally over, his only wish was to return to Camelot as quickly as possible, to see his friends and fellow knights, and let them know he was alive.

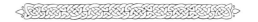

One chilly winter's afternoon, King Arthur was walking in the courtyard at Camelot when a tall, bearded knight, wearing rusty armor, came riding wearily across the drawbridge on a bony horse. Arthur noticed first a piece of tattered green silk tied around his arm and then, when the knight removed his helmet, a long, thin scar on the side of his neck.

"Greetings, noble knight. You look in need of a rest and some sustenance," Arthur said. Sir Gawain smiled.

"King Arthur and his knights welcome you to Camelot," the king went on. "Will you tell us your name?"

"You don't recognize me, do you?" replied Gawain. "My name is Sir Gawain, and I am proud to be able to call myself a Knight of the Round Table."

SIR TRISTRAM'S TALE

Just as Merlin had said, the seats around the Round Table were enchanted. Whenever a knight died, his name would fade from the back of his chair and whenever a new knight arrived, a new name would magically inscribe itself there instead.

The back of one of the chairs, though, had remained blank for so long that Arthur wondered if a new name would ever be written there. Knights came and went, and still the chair stayed empty, its gleaming, polished wood unmarked by any lettering. People said that the seat must be destined for an exceptionally noble occupant.

One day, however, as Lancelot was going to take his place at the table, he ran his hand along the back of the empty chair. He stopped and touched it again.

"The empty seat!" he called to King Arthur. "It's got an inscription on it!"

The other knights crowded around the chair, jostling to see the letters forming, ever clearer and deeper, before their eyes.

"What does it say?" called Gawain.

"Sir. . . Tris. . ." Lancelot read slowly. "Sir Trist. . . Sir Tristram!"

"Yes?"

Everyone turned around. There in the doorway was the silhouette of a tall, well-built young man with thick, curly hair. He had no horse or armor, but carried a wooden harp in his left hand, and a small bundle of possessions in his right.

"Were you expecting me?" he asked.

When Sir Tristram had been ushered to his seat, and given some food and wine, the other knights started questioning him.

"Where have you come from?" asked Sir Lancelot. "Who are your parents?" Sir Kay wanted to know. "And, if it's not a rude question," said King Arthur, "where are your weapons, your horse and squire, your shield?"

The handsome young man smiled wistfully. "I'll tell you my story," he said, "and how I came to be a poor wandering traveler. It's a sad tale."

"I was born in France," said Tristram. "My father was King Meliodas of Lyonesse, and my mother was Elizabeth, the sister of King Mark of Cornwall. Soon after I was born," said Tristram sadly, "my mother died, and as she was dying, she told her maid to name me Tristram, which means 'sadness'.

"But I had a happy childhood. Except for a mother, I had all I could wish for. When I was seven, I was sent to live with

Gouvernale, an old friend of my father's. He taught me everything ~ how to ride and shoot with a bow, how to use a sword and a lance, and also how to play the harp. Later, Gouvernale became my loyal servant. He even saved my life. But I'll come to that," said Tristram with a smile.

"Anyway, by the time I was seventeen, I had grown into a big lad and I was good at fighting. I wasn't a knight yet, but everyone said I should go on a journey of some sort, to see the world. It was decided that I should visit my uncle, King Mark.

"I'll always remember the day I left home," said Tristram, gazing into the distance. "The sun was glittering on the waves in the harbor. There was a fresh wind. Everything was loaded into the ship. I had it all; the best that money could buy ~ a wonderful horse, new armor, a painted shield, and a sword that had been specially made for the occasion. My father was so proud of me.

"And then, when it was all packed, we set off ~ me, Gouvernale and the crew. My father stood on the dockside waving until he was just a tiny speck, and all I could see was the sun glinting on his crown.

"Well," said Tristram, turning away from his happy memories. "What a rude awakening I had, when we got to Cornwall. There was I, sweet and innocent, raised in a warm and happy land. I marched straight into King Mark's castle to introduce myself, and the first thing I knew, Gouvernale and I were arrested and thrown into the dungeons!

" 'You don't just wander into King Mark's castle unannounced,' snarled a bullying knight, Sir Sneap, who had been sent to interrogate us. 'You could be Irish spies.'

" 'I am Prince Tristram of Lyonesse!' I told him indignantly, 'and King Mark is my uncle!' In the end, it was only because I looked so much like my poor mother, his sister Elizabeth, that Mark believed me and let me stay. At that time, the whole place was in turmoil. They didn't trust anyone. They were constantly on the lookout. Those were dark days."

"Why didn't they trust anyone?" asked Sir Gawain.

"It was the threat from Ireland," said Tristram. "King Angwish had demanded tribute money from Mark. Mark had refused. Now, Angwish was threatening to send his best and most frightening knight, Sir Marhault, to Cornwall. Unless a Cornish knight could beat Marhault in hand-to-hand combat, Angwish was going to declare war."

"And did the knight turn up?"

"Yes, he did. He camped on an island off the Cornish coast, and he challenged Mark to find someone to fight against him. He gave Mark three weeks ~ after that he was going to return to Ireland and tell King Angwish the war was on.

"Of course, Mark was in a terrible state. Most of his knights weren't really very good, unfortunately. Marhault, on the other hand, was a monster. He was at least seven feet tall, and very mean. And there was also a rumour that Marhault's sister, the Queen of Ireland, was something of a sorceress. Everyone was worried that Marhault had been made even more powerful by magic, and no one wanted to go near him.

"In the end, when there were just two days to go, I decided to volunteer. I fancied my chances ~ I knew I was better than any of Mark's knights. When I told Gouvernale, he looked sad, but resigned, as if he'd known this was coming.

" 'I'd hate to lose you,' he said. 'And your father. . . he'd be devastated. But,' he added, 'you've got to start somewhere, I suppose. And if you remember everything I've taught you, you'll be in with a chance.'

"All that remained was to persuade Mark to make me a knight, and I would be ready. He didn't hesitate ~ the ceremony was performed at once. He sent Marhault a message, and the next thing I knew, Gouvernale and I were sailing across to the island where the Irish knight had set up camp.

"I got off the boat with my horse, and Gouvernale tightened all my armor. I could see that he was crying, but he was trying to hide it. 'Good luck, Tristram,' he choked. 'You'll be fine. You'll do me proud, I know.' I think he was trying to convince himself as much as me. Then he got back in the boat and waited for the fight to begin.

"Marhault was waiting for me. He was sitting on a big, shaggy, dark brown horse, armed to the teeth, with his lance pointing straight at me. As soon as I was in position, he set off, galloping toward me with his head down. He was going so fast that when we crashed into each other, both our lances shattered. I found myself face down on the grass, and when I got up, he was running at me with his sword. I quickly drew mine.

"But it was as much as I could do to deflect his blows. He chased me around the island, swiping at me with his blade, until I was exhausted. Occasionally, as I ran around, I could see Gouvernale sitting in the little boat, with his hands clapped over his eyes.

"To be honest, I was no match for Marhault," Tristram admitted. "It was only because of luck, and his own arrogance, that he didn't kill me."

"What happened?" said Arthur.

"Well, finally he landed a huge blow on my thigh. It cut through my armor and deep into my leg, and I fell. I was crippled and pouring with blood, I couldn't get up, and I was sure he was going to kill me.

"Instead, he started laughing scornfully. 'You pathetic little worm!' he snorted. 'You thought you could take on Marhault, the mighty knight of Ireland, did you? Well, let me tell you something, you *amateur*. My blade is coated in poison, made by my sister Queen Isaud. You'll never recover from that wound! Hah hah hah!'

"His words infuriated me. I had been ready to die, but now I forced myself up, and before he knew what was happening I struck him on top of the head. My sword sliced through his helmet and went right into his skull. He fell to his knees, groaning, and I pulled my sword out and left him lying there."

"Was he dead?" asked Gawain eagerly.

"No. But when I looked at my bloodstained sword I saw that a little piece of it was missing. A fragment had broken off and become embedded in his brain, and I knew that, eventually, it would kill him. But when his servants took him back to Ireland, he was still alive."

"And what about you?" Arthur persisted. "How did you survive the poison?"

"It was agony," said Tristram, wincing at the memory. "I was put to bed to recover,

. . .he set off, galloping toward me. . .

and my other cuts and scratches healed, but that wound on my thigh stayed open and raw. If anyone touched it, it burned with excruciating pain. And all the time, I was growing weaker and weaker.

"All the doctors in Mark's kingdom were summoned, but none of them could help. Until one day an Irish maiden, who was passing by, heard about my plight, and she offered her advice. She said that if the poison came from Ireland, I would have to go to Ireland to have it cured. In fact, the person who had made the poison would probably be the only one who could heal me.

"Well, I'm sure you can imagine how I took that news. How could I possibly ask

Queen Isaud to heal me, after I'd struck her own brother on the head?

"But Gouvernale came up with a plan. He decided that we should dress up as minstrels, and go to Ireland in disguise to look for a cure. Both of us could play the harp, after all. So my wound was bandaged up, and we dressed ourselves in musicians' costumes. I renamed myself Tramtris, the traveling minstrel, and Gouvernale called himself Vernalgo. King Mark lent us a ship. As soon as everything was ready, I

limped down to the harbor, supported by my faithful friend ~ and off we sailed."

"In Ireland, we went down a treat. They'd never heard the music of Lyonesse before, and they loved it. We were invited to play at festivals, weddings and feasts ~ and no one guessed I was really a king's son.

"Then one day, the message we'd been waiting for arrived at our lodgings. It was brought by a grandly dressed messenger on a gold-bridled horse, and it read:

The King and Queen request the
presence of the famed musicians,
Tramtris and Vernalgo,
to perform at their Christmas Feast.
RSVP

"Well, we practiced like demons for that performance. Hour after hour, late into the night, Gouvernale and I rehearsed the loveliest tunes we knew, perfecting every note and trill. When the great day came ~ although I say so myself ~ we were by far the best entertainers at the feast, although they had jugglers, fire-eaters and dancers too. I noticed that the queen in particular was entranced, and during the encore I took care to smile sweetly at her.

"After the feast, all the performers were summoned before King Angwish and Queen Isaud, as was traditional. Some were rewarded with golden rings, some with jeweled bracelets and caskets. When it was my turn, and I limped up to the throne with Gouvernale behind me, Queen Isaud looked at me kindly. 'You and your friend were our favorite performers this evening,' she said. 'You may name your own reward.'

"I didn't need to be asked twice ~ I was still in agony with my wound. 'I have heard great things about your majesty's healing powers,' I began, politely. 'And as my reward, I would beg you to heal my wound, which has troubled me for many months.'

"The queen looked a little taken aback, but she gladly agreed. It was what came next that startled me. King Angwish leaned forward, as if he had something very important to say.

" 'We also have a special surprise for you, Tramtris,' he announced. 'From this day onward, we would like you and Vernalgo to be our permanent court musicians.' He beamed broadly, and I smiled and thanked him, but my mind was in turmoil. How could I stay here, under an assumed name, and never see my uncle or father again? I had no desire to be a harp player for ever ~ even a royal harp player!

"But we could hardly refuse. It was a great honor to be asked, and I was also desperate to have my leg healed, so we accepted as graciously as possible."

"And the queen healed you?" asked Sir Gawain.

"She certainly did," said Tristram. "The very next day, she examined the gash on my leg. I was worried she'd ask me how I got it, and why it hadn't healed, but instead she just mixed up some kind of herbal ointment, applied it to the wound, and within a week I was as good as new.

"Gouvernale and I thought we'd better stay for a while, until we'd decided what to do. We thought that after a decent interval, like a year, we could make up an excuse and leave. So, meanwhile, we lived as court minstrels. We had beautiful quarters in the castle, whatever we wanted to eat and drink, and we only had to work a few hours a week. But that wasn't the best thing." A dreamy expression passed across Tristram's face.

"What was?" asked Lancelot curiously.

"Iseult," whispered Tristram, gazing wistfully into space. "The princess. One of my tasks was to teach her to play the harp. She was *so* gorgeous. And kind, and funny, and intelligent," he said. "Before long, we weren't paying too much attention to the music. We spent most of our time together flirting. I loved her. . . And I still do," Tristram added quietly. "But of course I couldn't tell her who I was. We had to keep our love secret ~ she would never have been allowed to marry the court minstrel. It was heartbreaking.

"Gouvernale thought I was completely mad. He kept warning me I was taking a huge risk ~ if I was found out, I'd probably be executed. Well, I needn't have worried about *that*. We fell out of favor soon enough.

"I used to practice swordfighting with Gouvernale in my spare time. My beautiful sword was the only weapon I'd brought with me. Well, one day after we'd been practicing, I decided to take a bath. Gouvernale filled the tub with hot water for me, and I got in.

"I was lying there, relaxing and admiring the tiles on the ceiling, when all of a sudden I heard an awful, blood-chilling scream of rage. The door flew open, and there stood Queen Isaud. In her right hand

was my sword, which I must have left lying outside my chamber. And in her left hand was a little sliver of metal.

" 'Traitor!' she screamed. 'Impostor! Liar! MURDERER!' I sat up, splashing water everywhere.

" 'Is there a problem, your majesty?' I said, trying to sound as calm as possible, but I was trembling.

" '*Problem*?' she roared. 'Yes, I should think there is something of a *problem* with you being *Tristram*, the knight who killed my brother! Look!' And she held up the sword and the fragment of metal, and fitted them together perfectly.

" 'Your majesty, I. . . I. . .'

"I had no excuse. I was done for.

" 'I think you know where I found *this*, don't you?' she fumed, marching right up to the bathtub and thrusting the fragment under my nose. I quickly grabbed a towel to wrap around myself. 'IN MY BROTHER'S BRAIN!' she shrieked. 'After he died a slow and agonizing DEATH! And guess whose SWORD it came from? Well, *Tramtris* the minstrel,' she sneered, 'I think I've got another little job for this sword.'

"And with that she heaved the weapon high above her head, ready to slice me in half. I cowered in the bathtub, waiting for the fatal blow.

"Just then, footsteps came rushing across the tiled floor. Someone grabbed the queen from behind and wrestled her to the ground.

" 'Gouvernale,' I breathed. I leaped out of the bath and grabbed the sword, just in time to see the castle guards pouring into the room.

"Well, after that, we fully expected to be hung, drawn and quartered. We were brought before King Angwish, bound in chains, for him to make his judgment.

"His twinkly old eyes looked me up and down. 'So,' he said, sounding almost impressed, 'You are Tristram, the slayer of Sir Marhault.' I confessed that I was.

" 'And the son of King Meliodas of Lyonesse,' he went on. 'An old comrade of mine. Perhaps you'd like to tell me how you came here.'

"So I told him the whole story ~ about my upbringing, how I came to Cornwall, and how my fight with Sir Marhault had been my first battle.

" 'I was only defending my uncle's kingdom, your majesty,' I pleaded. Then I told him how I had needed a cure for my wound, and how we'd disguised ourselves as musicians and come to Ireland.

" 'I can see that you're an intelligent young man and a valiant knight,' King Angwish announced, 'and it would be an awful shame to have to execute you. But as I'm sure you understand, my wife can't be expected to welcome you. She's had a terrible shock, and is still mourning her dear brother. So,' he sighed, 'I'm banishing you both from Ireland.' He smiled kindly. 'You have twenty-four hours to leave.'

" 'Thank you!' I fell to my knees. 'Your majesty, thank you a thousand times for sparing my life. If there's ever anything I can do for you. . .'

" 'Perhaps we'll meet again,' said the king wisely. 'And I'll remember your kind offer. I'll miss you both, and your beautiful playing,' he added generously.

"So," said Tristram, taking a swig of wine from his goblet, "that was how we left Ireland. I bade Iseult a secret farewell, and we returned to King Mark's court.

"But all was not well in Cornwall. Mark was under the influence of the evil Sir Sneap; and Sneap didn't take kindly to me being Mark's favorite. He was worried I might inherit the throne, as Mark had no children. So he started urging Mark to find a wife.

"That was when I wished I'd kept my big mouth shut. When Gouvernale and I had told the story of our travels, I'd gone on and on about the beautiful, charming Princess Iseult of Ireland. So Mark decided he wanted to marry *her*. 'It's an excellent idea,' he congratulated himself. 'It will secure peace between Cornwall and Ireland.'

"Worst of all, he wanted *me* to go to Ireland for him and ask for Iseult's hand. I tried to remind him that I'd been banished, but he had his heart set on Iseult. 'Angwish obviously likes you,' he said. 'I'm sure you can win him round.'

"And that's how Gouvernale and I found ourselves on another boat to Ireland, dressed in our own clothes this time, along with our armor and horses," Tristram explained. "I had no idea how to approach King Angwish or what to say to him ~ I was sure we'd be thrown out at once. And how on earth would we avoid the queen?

"But, yet again, luck was on our side. The ship was blown off course in a heavy storm, and we ended up stuck in North Wales, the kingdom of King Ryon."

"Doesn't sound too lucky to me," mumbled King Arthur.

"There was nothing to do until the storm died down, so we headed inland to look around. And soon enough, we came across a tournament. It was a big one, with lots of knights, pavilions everywhere, trumpet-playing and feasting.

"Just as the games were about to begin, there was a commotion. A pair of brothers called Sir Blamour and Sir Bleoberys had arrived, and they didn't look too friendly. They announced that someone at the tournament had done them wrong.

" 'King Angwish of Ireland,' Sir Blamour shouted, 'killed my cousin Sir Bogue. Where are you, Angwish?' he yelled. 'Come out and fight!' "

"You mean Angwish was at the tournament?" interrupted Gawain.

"Yes, it turned out he was ~ as a spectator," said Tristram. "Well, he came forward and said that he *had* killed Sir Bogue, years and years before in an honest fight ~ and he was far too old to have a battle now. He pleaded with the brothers, but they insisted.

"That was when I spotted my chance. I rode up to the platform and said that I was Sir Tristram, and I would be delighted to fight Sir Blamour on King Angwish's behalf.

"He was as surprised as anyone to see me, but he was in no position to refuse. So the first fight of the day was between me and Sir Blamour.

"He was a big knight, and a strong challenger. It was a close-run thing. We charged together, and both of us got badly bruised when the blow knocked us off our horses. Then we dueled for over an hour, and it seemed neither of us would win ~ but finally, the trusty sword my father had made for me proved the stronger. As our weapons smashed against each other for the hundredth time, Sir Blamour's blade suddenly shattered. I chased him, overcame him and pinned him to the ground, with my sword at his throat. There was a huge cheer, and I was declared the winner.

"Then King Angwish came over, helped Sir Blamour to his feet, and shook hands with him and his brother in front of everyone. When they had all made their peace, he turned back to me.

" 'You've saved my life, Sir Tristram,' he said. 'I could never have been a match for Sir Blamour.'

" 'Well,' I admitted, 'I did owe you a favor. You saved my life too.'

" 'Please,' King Angwish offered, 'come home with me after the tournament, and be my guests again. The queen is much better, and I'm sure she'll welcome you when she hears what's happened.'

"So, you can see how fate has favored me," said Sir Tristram. "In Ireland, when I cautiously asked whether Iseult was married yet, Angwish seemed delighted.

" 'I've been hoping you would ask about that!' he said excitedly. 'Isaud and I have agreed you'd make the perfect husband for our daughter!'

"It was painful to have to explain that I wasn't asking to marry Iseult myself, but was on orders from King Mark and could not betray him, even though I admired Iseult deeply. Eventually, Angwish agreed that a marriage between Mark and Iseult would secure peace, and it was arranged for her to accompany us back to Cornwall.

"Iseult wasn't very happy about it, but she had to obey her father. And I tried to console myself. At least I would have her delightful company for the journey, and I would see her regularly at Mark's castle ~ even if she couldn't be my own wife."

"Indeed," interposed Sir Lancelot, gazing, somewhat obviously, at Guinevere.

"The day of our departure came, and I helped the beautiful princess aboard our ship, along with her faithful maid Brangwain.

"What I hadn't realized was that Queen Isaud, with her knowledge of herbs, had prepared a love potion. She could see that Iseult and I liked each other, and she couldn't bear to think of her daughter being unhappy with King Mark. So she'd given Brangwain a bottle of the potion to give to Iseult and Mark when they were married.

"Iseult and I knew nothing of this as we sat on the deck in the sunshine, admiring the blue-green waters of the Irish Sea, and secretly holding hands. Since we'd set off, Brangwain had been seasick, and spent all her time in her cabin. Gouvernale was busy managing the crew, and Iseult and I were free to enjoy a few days alone together. We reassured each other that we would still be friends. Mark was quite old, we agreed. Perhaps, when he died, we would be able to get married.

"And with these secret thoughts we calmed ourselves, and prepared for our arrival in Cornwall.

"One evening, as the sun was going down, I went in search of something for Iseult and me to drink. Lying in a basket outside Brangwain's cabin was a dark brown bottle, stoppered with a crumbly old cork. It looked just like one of the wine bottles from Angwish's castle, so of course I assumed it must be part of the provisions Brangwain had brought along for her mistress to use on the journey. I took the bottle and two goblets, and returned to Iseult.

" 'To you, Iseult,' I toasted her as we raised our cups. 'It won't be all that bad.'

" 'To a long and happy friendship,' Iseult agreed. We drank.

"But when we looked up from our goblets, our eyes met like magnets drawn together. Although we had just decided we'd be happy enough as friends, suddenly we were filled with passion for each other. Iseult threw down her cup and ran into my arms.

" 'Oh, *no*, my *dear*!' said a matronly voice behind her. 'I *knew* I should have kept it in my cabin. Oh my goodness. What *is* the queen going to say?' Brangwain scurried over to the empty bottle. She turned it upside-down and shook it. Then she looked up at us, her eyes filled with sadness."

"So what happened in Cornwall?" asked Sir Gawain.

"Iseult married Mark," said Tristram. "She had to. We were so in love, we both wept at the wedding. But for a long time, Mark didn't realize what was going on. In fact, it all might have worked out if it weren't for Sir Sneap," glowered Tristram, bitterly.

"What happened?" asked Lancelot.

"Iseult and I did remain great friends," Tristram went on, "and we tried not to let our relationship go any further. I knew I would be exiled, at the very least, if I was caught betraying Mark.

"But one day, Mark's squire was ill. While he was off work, Mark asked me to get the queen from her chambers. I never usually went near them ~ it would have been too risky. But as Mark had sent me, I thought I would be safe from suspicion.

"I knocked on the door of Iseult's chamber, and when she opened it, she was looking more lovely than ever. The morning sunlight was streaming through the golden silk curtains in her room, and her face glowed with joy when she saw me. Before we could stop ourselves, we were in each other's arms, and I was kissing her passionately.

"It was a stupid thing to do. Because immediately, out of the shadows behind me stepped Sir Sneap. It turned out he'd arranged the whole thing ~ he'd persuaded Mark to send me to the queen's quarters, and then he'd lain in wait, watching to see what we would do. He called the guards and I was arrested, despite Iseult's protestations.

"And that's how I found myself cast out forever from my uncle's kingdom," Tristram concluded sadly. "Cruelly banished, with no time for farewells, from my beloved lady. I barely had time to grab my harp and a few possessions. And because I am a bold knight, I decided to come here and ask you, King Arthur, if I could begin a new life at Camelot.

"Although," added Sir Tristram, remembering the name inscribed on his seat, "this chair seems to have accepted me already."

"And you are a worthy addition to our ranks," smiled Arthur. "Welcome, Sir Tristram, to the Round Table."

CHAPTER EIGHT

THE ENCHANTED SHIP

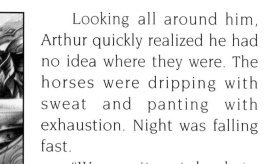

"**F**aster!" yelled King Arthur. It was a fine summer's afternoon and the knights were pounding through Camelot Forest at breakneck speed, in pursuit of an enormous stag. The terrified creature was crashing through the under-growth ahead of them, wrenching off whole branches with its antlers in a frantic bid to escape. Charging after it came the knights, spurring on their horses over logs, through mud and across streams, deeper and deeper into the dark and tangled forest.

Arthur soon found himself out in front, with Sir Uriens and Sir Accolon following close behind him. Their quarry was still well within sight when they reached the other side of the forest and galloped out into the bright sunshine. Mile after mile they rode in the hazy heat of the afternoon, up hills and across valleys, over thick hedgerows and through meadows until they reached the banks of a wide, green river. There they came to an abrupt halt. The stag had disappeared.

Looking all around him, Arthur quickly realized he had no idea where they were. The horses were dripping with sweat and panting with exhaustion. Night was falling fast.

"We can't get back to Camelot tonight," said Arthur, dismounting. "We'll have to find somewhere to shelter." So they started walking wearily along the riverbank in the twilight, leading their horses behind them.

"What's that?" said Uriens all of a sudden, pointing down the mist-covered river. Peering through the gloom, Arthur could just about make out a large, dark shape in the distance. It was gliding toward them, parting the fog as it cut through the muddy, green water.

The three men stood transfixed on the riverbank, gazing at the looming shape as it drifted nearer and nearer, to the sound of strange, ethereal music.

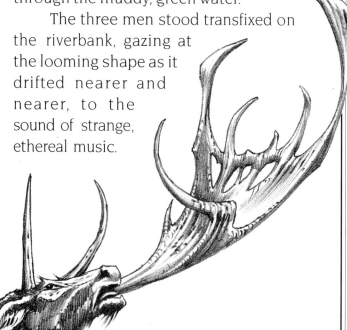

"A beautiful ship," gasped Sir Uriens, as the vessel sailed closer.

"A ship!" said Accolon, squinting in the dim light. "A beautiful ship," gasped Uriens, as the vessel sailed closer. Now they could see the ornate carvings and gold that decorated its hull. Its sails billowed gently in the warm candlelight that spilled from its cabins. Soft laughter and singing filled the air as the ship floated toward the riverbank.

"Come in, good knights," called a voice from inside, as a wooden walkway was lowered onto the bank. The tired and hungry men needed little encouragement. They immediately tethered their horses, crossed the walkway and stepped on board.

Twelve beautiful faces smiled at them when they entered the cabin. Twelve graceful pairs of hands reached out to help them pull off their mud-spattered gauntlets and boots.

"Who are you, fair ladies?" asked Uriens when they were seated at a long table with an enormous feast spread out in front of them.

"We are the damsels of the river," sang the twelve women in unison.

"This must be magic," whispered Accolon to Arthur. "Do you think it's safe?"

"I'm not sure ~ it could be a trick," said Arthur. His head started to spin. Accolon's face was going in and out of focus. Accolon was also having trouble staying awake.

"This wine . . . it's making me feel very strange," he said, drowsily.

"I think it's . . ." The laughter and music faded as his head hit the table.

Sir Accolon was awakened by somebody kicking him in the leg.

"Get up, get up mister knight,
Get up, get up for a fight.
Get up, get up, now it's light,
Get up, get up, time to fight,"

said an urgent little voice in his ear. Accolon opened his eyes. The voice belonged to a dwarf who was turning perfect cartwheels on the grass in front of him as he chanted his rhyme over and over again. At the end of each verse he ran over and kicked Accolon.

"I don't think you'll ever be a minstrel," yawned Accolon, raising his head.

"Well, I did want to be a knight," said the dwarf, "but in the end I had to settle for fool, because nobody would take me seriously and I couldn't afford the armor."

None of this made sense to Accolon. He'd fallen asleep in a magic ship, and woken up in a field with a dwarf gibbering in his ear. It was all too much before breakfast.

"Where am I and what do you

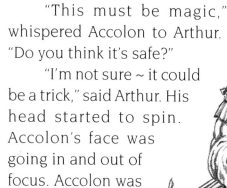

want?" he said bluntly, brushing grass from his legs.

"You've got to fight, mister knight, now it's light. . ."

"Yes all right, all right, I've got that part, but when and where, and who?"

"Whom is the pronoun you require," said the dwarf.

"Don't be facetious and answer the question," snapped Accolon.

"Oh very well ~ tomorrow morning, here, Sir Damas, hand-to-hand combat, usual stuff. Here's a sword and scabbard, present from Morgan le Fay." And he thrust an exquisitely decorated sword into Accolon's hand.

"But I recognize that sword. . ." said Accolon.

"Of course you do," said the dwarf. "Now follow me."

Sir Uriens woke up back at Camelot, next to his wife, Morgan le Fay. He was confused.

"I thought I was on a ship miles from here," he mumbled.

"It must have been a dream, my dear. Now go back to sleep," whispered Morgan.

Arthur was awakened by water dripping onto his nose and trickling slowly down his neck. He then became aware that he had a terrible headache, that his throat was parched and that there was something very wrong with his arms. They wouldn't move.

Opening his eyes, he discovered why. He was chained to a wall in the darkest, dankest dungeon imaginable. His legs were clamped in irons and his armor was nowhere to be seen. But worst of all, Excalibur was gone!

"So it *was* a trick," he murmured, suddenly remembering the enchanted ship and the damsels of the river. In the dim light of the dreadful dungeon his eyes began to register a gruesome spectacle.

Dozens of other men were chained to the walls around him. Some were groaning, and some were so thin that they looked like little more than skin-covered skeletons.

"What am I doing here?" he asked hoarsely.

"Waiting to die," croaked the man next to him. Then, one by one, all the other prisoners related their stories. They told him that they were all captives of an evil knight called Sir Damas, who had seized his brother's castle and land after the death of their father. The brother, an honest knight by the name of Sir Ontzlake, had challenged Damas to a fight in order to settle the matter. But Damas was too cowardly to accept the challenge himself, so he was in the habit of capturing wandering knights and offering them the choice of fighting in his place, or imprisonment for life.

Sir Damas was so despised that every single knight so far had chosen to be imprisoned. Some had been captives for years and years. Eighteen had already perished from starvation or disease.

"But I have to get out of this godforsaken place!" screamed Arthur, tugging desperately at his bonds.

"There is no escape," said a feeble voice from the corner.

"Except in a coffin," said his grim-faced neighbor.

"If the rats don't get you first," added another, mournfully.

At that moment the heavy door of the dungeon creaked open and a young, fresh-faced woman bustled in. Arthur said he thought he recognized her as one of Morgan le Fay's maids, but she denied all knowledge of the sorceress. She said she had brought a message from Sir Damas, and offered Arthur the choice of fighting for the evil knight or staying imprisoned for the rest of his life ~ just as the other prisoners had described.

"If I have to choose, I'd rather die fighting than starve to death in this dismal place!" said Arthur, surveying once again the gloomy dungeon and its miserable occupants. Suddenly he had an idea: "Tell Sir Damas I'll only fight for him if all my fellow prisoners are released, whatever the outcome of the fight, and if I can have a well-wrought sword and shield and a decent suit of armor."

The maid immediately called two guards, who unchained Arthur and took him up to meet Sir Damas.

"I'll agree to your conditions," said the evil knight in a wheedling nasal drone, "but only if you promise to fight to the death."

"I promise," said Arthur.

Meanwhile, Accolon was following the dwarf to the home of Sir Ontzlake. The dwarf chattered as they walked, running ahead every so often to turn a few cartwheels and chant a few more rhymes.

He explained that Accolon was to fight Sir Damas for Morgan le Fay. The sword would ensure that Accolon won, and then he would become king and she would be queen.

Accolon agreed to this willingly. During his time at Camelot he and Morgan le Fay had fallen in love, even though she was married to Sir Uriens. Accolon didn't know exactly what the sorceress was planning, but this chance to please her was too good to miss.

When they at last arrived, Sir Ontzlake was outside to greet them.

"Welcome to my humble abode," he said, hobbling toward them. "You've arrived in good time."

"For what?" asked Accolon.

"For the fight," said Ontzlake. "You see, I've just heard that my lily-livered brother, Sir Damas, has at last agreed to settle our differences in the traditional way ~ hand-to-hand combat at dawn. But as you can see, I'm in no state to fight ~ wounded in both thighs, as luck would have it."

"So I am here in order to fight this battle instead of you?" said Accolon.

"Indeed," replied Ontzlake, "but if you wear my white armor and ride my horse, nobody will know the difference. Damas is a coward, and a terrible fighter. You should have no problem killing him, especially with that fine sword."

"Killing him?"

"It's a fight to the death," said Ontzlake. "Didn't I mention that?"

"To the death," repeated Accolon slowly. The dwarf chuckled and ran off across the meadows.

Very early the next morning, before it was even light, Arthur heard a knock on the door of the chamber where he had been trying to sleep. In fact, he had spent most of the night worrying about how he was going to kill Sir Ontzlake without his magic sword.

"Come in!" he called.

The maid who had come to the dungeon the day before stepped into the room and thrust a package into his hands.

"Morgan le Fay sends you this with her love," the maid said, and scuttled out.

Arthur quickly unwrapped the long bundle, ripping open the strings that bound its familiar shape.

"Excalibur!" he cried, clutching the gleaming scabbard. He'd no idea how his half-sister had retrieved the sword or smuggled it to him, but it had come just in time. With Excalibur he would defeat Ontzlake and the magic scabbard would ensure he lost no blood, however ferocious the fight.

He quickly put on the black armor that Sir Damas had provided, and strapped the sword to his side. Just as the sun was rising, he galloped out of the gates to do battle with Sir Ontzlake.

A large crowd had gathered to watch the long-awaited clash of the brothers. The two knights, one in black and one in white, arrived from opposite ends of the meadow, both with their visors clamped firmly down so that their faces could not be seen.

They strode purposefully toward one another and stood face to face in the middle of the field. Then each knight reached down to his side, drew his sword and raised it high in the air. The crowd gasped. The razor-sharp blades that sparkled in the sun were identical!

With a great groan that rang around the battlefield. . .

. . .the knights clashed their swords together. . .

With a great groan that rang around the battlefield, the knights clashed their swords together and a frenzied fight to the death began. Blow was exchanged for blow, strike for strike, and yell for yell as they battled through the morning. To Arthur's surprise, each blow from the white knight's sword pierced his armor and cut his flesh. But each strike from his own blade failed to have an effect.

The spectators gasped and cheered. They'd never seen such a splendidly savage duel. Sir Damas, far from being a coward, as they had been led to believe, was extraordinarily brave, fighting on with a useless sword and a damaged suit of armor, while his brother brought blow after blow raining down on his head.

Oblivious to the roar of the crowd, and dizzy with pain, Arthur suddenly staggered backward and fell to his knees. He lowered his head and saw blood gushing from his wounds onto the grass.

Why was the scabbard not protecting him? And what was wrong with Excalibur?

His opponent was now towering over him, about to deliver another blow that would probably be the last. Clenching his teeth and screaming with agony, Arthur summoned just enough strength to raise his sword to deflect the blow. As the two swords clashed again, he felt his own blade shatter into smithereens.

This was not Excalibur! Before his opponent could strike again, he had cast what was left of the weapon to the ground in fury, and struggled to his feet.

"Surrender, Sir Damas," taunted the white knight, "or die!"

"I'll fight to the death," growled Arthur.

Then he lowered his head, raised his shield and charged at the knight, ramming his whole weight into his opponent's stomach and knocking him over.

The white knight's sword flew from his hand as he fell sprawling on the grass. Arthur grabbed it. The moment his hand touched the handle, he knew it was the real Excalibur. His eyes darted over to the scabbard, still hanging at the white knight's side. He wrenched it off and flung it far from the fight.

"Now it's your turn for a taste of Excalibur," he shouted. He tore off the white knight's helmet, raised Excalibur and struck as hard as he could. Then he looked down. In an instant he recognized the blood-covered face that stared up at him.

"Sir Accolon!" he cried and ripped off his own helmet.

"King Arthur?" whispered Accolon.

"So you stole Excalibur!"

"No!" moaned Accolon, grimacing with pain. "It was Morgan le Fay. I promise. She sent it to me. . . after her damsels put us to sleep on the ship." Accolon was fighting for breath. "She said I should fight for her. . . but I didn't know I had to fight you. I thought you were Sir Damas."

"And I thought you were Ontzlake," said Arthur, kneeling beside him. "She tricked both of us! She put me in Damas's dungeon until I agreed to fight. . . and sent me a fake Excalibur. I trusted her, but she wanted me dead!"

Arthur vowed that he would get his revenge on Morgan le Fay. Little did he know that even as they spoke, she was carrying out the next stage of her evil plot at Camelot.

CHAPTER NINE

THE SCHEMING SORCERESS

Morgan le Fay was awakened by bright sunshine streaming through a crack in the curtains and onto her face. Sir Uriens was snoring peacefully beside her.

"Still dead to the world, dear?" she whispered. "Good."

Taking care not to disturb him, she eased herself out of the bed, crept across the chamber and out of the door. It was still very early. Apart from a few maids, no one at Camelot was awake. She had plenty of time.

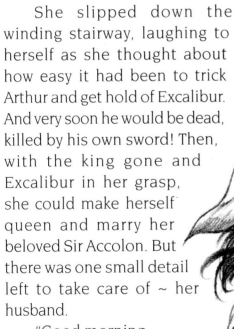

She slipped down the winding stairway, laughing to herself as she thought about how easy it had been to trick Arthur and get hold of Excalibur. And very soon he would be dead, killed by his own sword! Then, with the king gone and Excalibur in her grasp, she could make herself queen and marry her beloved Sir Accolon. But there was one small detail left to take care of ~ her husband.

"Good morning, my lady."

The maid's cheerful voice startled her.

"Oh. . . er, good morning, Alice dear," said Morgan. "I was just on my way to find you. Could you pop over to the armory and bring me a sword? It's such a lovely morning, I thought I'd do a little sword practice before breakfast."

"Er. . . Yes, of course, my lady," said Alice, somewhat surprised. Her mistress seldom woke so early, nor spoke to her so politely. Nor did she usually show any interest in swords.

Alice scuttled off to the armory, collected the sword and delivered it to Morgan, but something about her mistress's behavior was still very worrying. Was it her agitation, her oddly exaggerated gestures when she took hold of the weapon, or the strange, almost sinister, glint in her eye? Alice began to suspect the worst. Her mistress was obviously about to kill herself, and she had to do something to stop her.

At that moment, the maid found herself right

outside Sir Uwain's chamber. He would know why his mother was acting so strangely. Without even stopping to knock, Alice burst in. Sir Uwain had just woken up.

"Sir, Sir, I'm sorry," she gabbled frantically, "I'm worried about my lady. . . She asked for a sword, and then she said she wanted to practice, but she's heading for the staircase, and I just thought. . ."

Before Alice could even finish her sentence, Uwain had jumped out of bed. He raced along the passage to his parents' chamber where his father was still sleeping, and hid behind the heavy curtains.

Seconds later he heard the door open, and peeping out from his hiding place, saw his mother sneak in. She tiptoed over to the bed, lifted the sword up over her husband's head, and was just about to strike when Uwain leaped out and grabbed her arms from behind.

"You wicked woman," he snarled. "How could you do this? If you weren't my own mother, I'd kill you now!"

"Please, please don't tell anyone, Uwain," begged Morgan in an urgent whisper. "I can't imagine what came over me. I must have been sleepwalking. This won't happen again for as long as I live. . . I promise." Sir Uriens was now beginning to stir.

"What's all the noise about?" he asked sleepily.

"Nothing, my dear," said Morgan sweetly. "We were just saying how peaceful you look when you're asleep." And she hurried out of the room, followed by Uwain.

"I beg you not to tell anyone," she said again, clutching desperately at her son's sleeve. "For the sake of our family, nobody must know."

Uwain was silent. He just stared at his mother with a shocked look on his face.

"Your story's very hard to believe," he said at last, "but I'll keep it a secret, for the sake of the family. And it must never happen again."

"It won't," said Morgan. "I promise."

Later that morning, a covered cart arrived at Camelot with a message for Morgan le Fay:

Excalibur is back with its rightful owner. Your plot has been discovered. Here is a gift from King Arthur to his sister, with his love.

Morgan gingerly lifted the cover and peeked inside. Then she let out a loud wail and covered her face with her hands. It was the body of Sir Accolon.

After the fight between Accolon and Arthur, the king had been carried to an abbey in the middle of the forest, where his wounds were treated by a skillful surgeon. It had been too late to save Sir Accolon. He had taken his last breath on the battlefield soon after his true identity had been revealed. Arthur dispatched his body back to Camelot for burial, together with the message for his half-sister.

Before taking leave of the battlefield himself, the king had ensured that the quarrel between Damas and Ontzlake was finally settled. He ordered Damas to hand over the castle and lands to his brother, and release all the imprisoned knights. Sir Ontzlake and the knights were overjoyed at this outcome and pledged their allegiance to Arthur. Sir Damas protested feebly, but he was far too cowardly to take any action.

When Morgan le Fay received Arthur's message, she wasted no time. She had to get Excalibur back before her brother could take his revenge. But first she had to find out where he was. Taking care to hide her grief and anger, she went straight to Queen Guinevere and asked in her sweetest voice if she could possibly visit Arthur.

"Of course," said Guinevere, knowing nothing of Morgan's trickery. "He's resting in the old abbey in the middle of the forest."

Morgan set off at once with an escort of men. She rode all night and reached the abbey at noon the following day.

"I'm King Arthur's sister," she said to the abbess on arrival. "I've come to see my poor, wounded brother."

"He's sleeping for the first time in three days," said the abbess. "Can you wait a little longer before you disturb him?"

"I just want to see him ~ I promise I won't wake him," Morgan replied.

The abbess led her to Arthur's room.

"You may leave us alone," said the sorceress. "I only want to watch over him for a while."

As soon as the abbess had left, Morgan crept over to the bed. Arthur was sound asleep, clutching Excalibur tightly by the blade. She didn't dare try to take it, in case he woke up. Instead, she started to ferret around the room, looking for the magic scabbard. Finally she saw it poking out from underneath Arthur's pillow. She placed her fingers carefully around the end and began to ease the scabbard out, very, very slowly. Just then, Arthur murmured and rolled over.

"Blast!" she cursed under her breath. Her hand was trapped under Arthur's head! She muttered a quick spell to ensure it was Guinevere's voice that Arthur heard and Guinevere's soft hand he felt patting his shoulder.

"Move over, my darling, you've fallen asleep on my hand," Morgan whispered. Arthur mumbled a sleepy apology and rolled over in the bed. Morgan le Fay whipped the scabbard out from under the pillow and hurried out. When she rode away from the abbey, nobody knew the scabbard was hidden under her cloak.

Arthur was furious when he woke up to discover that Morgan had visited the abbey while he slept, and that the magic scabbard was gone. He set off at once in pursuit of his sister, stopping for Sir Ontzlake on the way. They had not ridden far when they met a shepherd on the road.

"Have you seen a woman with jet black hair, riding with a group of armed men?" Arthur asked the man.

"They galloped past just a couple of minutes ago, Sir," said the shepherd. "Fast as the wind, they were. Scattered my sheep everywhere, and. . ." Without even stopping to thank the man, Arthur and Ontzlake shot off in the direction he had indicated.

Before long, they caught sight of the wicked sorceress in the distance, galloping along the shore of Lake Avalon at the head of her entourage. They were still too far away to see her take the scabbard from beneath her swirling cloak.

"If I can't have it, then nobody can," Morgan le Fay sneered, launching the scabbard high into the air. It soared across the sky and then plunged into the middle of the lake with a loud splash, sinking without a trace.

Morgan hurtled on along the shore, with Arthur and Ontzlake charging after her, up the mountainside, around a huge rock and into a steep-sided valley. There they came to a sudden halt.

Morgan le Fay had vanished!

"Where on earth is she?" wailed Arthur, looking wildly around. All he could see were scores of strangely shaped boulders in the valley below.

Confused and exhausted, the two knights gave up and set off dejectedly back toward Camelot.

The moment they were out of sight, one of the boulders let out a loud cackle and began to change back into human form. It was Morgan le Fay. As her spell wore off, the other rocks melted back into men on horseback.

Queen Guinevere was elated at her husband's safe return, and organized an elaborate feast in his honor. Arthur, though still weak and tired from his long ordeal, summoned just enough energy to tell the Knights of the Round Table all about his adventures. The knights were outraged when they heard about Morgan le Fay's evil plot to kill their king, and many swore to seek revenge.

Six days later, when Arthur had fully recovered, a maid arrived at Camelot saying that she had a gift for the king. She was shown into the great hall.

"Your sister sends you this as a peace offering, in the hope that you will find it in your heart to forgive her," the maid said, as she thrust toward him the most

All he could see were scores of strangely shaped boulders . . .

spectacular and expensive-looking cloak Arthur had ever seen.

"Isn't it marvellous!" exclaimed the queen. "What a magnificent present! You should try it on at once."

Arthur reached out, and was just about to take the cloak, when he suddenly had an idea.

"Let me see it on you first," he said to the maid.

"Oh no, no, Sir, I couldn't possibly wear this," she gabbled nervously. "This cloak is for someone else entirely. I mean, this cloak is meant for a king."

"But I insist," said Arthur, beckoning to two of his knights. "Come on. We'll help you put it on."

The two knights gently took the heavy cloak from the flustered young woman and placed it around her shoulders. Then they leaped back in surprise and amazement. The maid had burst into flames! In an instant she was no more than a pile of smouldering ashes on the floor.

The great hall fell silent. All eyes turned toward Arthur.

"That evil, cowardly, vicious, scheming serpent!"

he hissed, almost purple with rage. "So this is her idea of a peace offering! I've had enough of her trickery and her lies." He glanced around the hall to make sure that everybody was listening as he raised his voice to a thunderous roar that rattled the rafters and could be heard deep in the darkest dungeons of Camelot.

"Bear witness to my words, good knights. MORGAN LE FAY IS NO SISTER OF MINE! From this day on she is banished from my heart, my court and my kingdom."

Then, with his words still echoing around the room and the pile of ashes still smouldering on the cold stone floor, he strode straight across the great hall and out through the door.

"Forever!" he shouted at the top of his voice, before slamming the heavy wooden door behind him.

CHAPTER TEN

SIR ORFEO

Sir Orfeo was the leader of the small Kingdom of Kent, which lay at the south-eastern tip of Britain, next to the Kingdom of Logres. It was a beautiful land, with gleaming white cliffs, pebbly beaches and rich, luscious meadows.

As well as being a much-loved ruler, Sir Orfeo was a great harpist, and he welcomed all musicians into his home. For years, young fiddle-players and drummers, singers and bagpipe players had come to Orfeo's castle to learn their trade. After dinner every evening, Orfeo would take up his harp and join the musicians, and his wife Heurodis, whom he loved with all his heart, would sing for the assembled company.

The morning after one such night of feasting and music-making, Lady Heurodis woke up with a headache and a sore throat. It had been a particularly late and rowdy evening. Merlett, Sir Orfeo's deputy, had been celebrating his birthday, and everyone had stayed up until the early hours, dancing and drinking wine. Heurodis had sung until her voice was hoarse.

The sun was already high in the sky, flooding the fields with warmth and sending sunbeams streaming through the leaves of the trees in the orchard.

That was the place to be, Heurodis decided, gazing out of the bedroom window.

She would call her maids and take a picnic to the orchard.

"Wasn't it a wonderful party last night?" giggled Grace, Heurodis's lady-in-waiting, as they made their way across the meadow. "I think Merlett enjoyed himself!"

"He never stopped for a minute!" exclaimed Millie, the maid who was carrying the picnic basket. "He was drinking and dancing all night!"

"I think *he'll* have a headache this morning too," laughed Heurodis, as she unlatched the heavy iron gate. As soon as they were inside the orchard, the rich, intoxicating scent of apple and pear blossom surrounded them, and the dry, soft, mossy grass felt like a velvet carpet under their feet.

After they had devoured some raspberries and cream, a whole pie and a bottle of pear juice, Heurodis decided she would read for a while. She leaned against the trunk of a pear tree and opened her leather-bound book.

But now that her head was feeling better, Heurodis could hardly stay awake. The warm sun, the sweet blossom-scent, and the restful sound of the birds singing made her deliciously drowsy. The book soon dropped from her hand onto the grass, and she slipped into a deep, relaxing sleep.

"Doesn't she look lovely?" whispered Millie admiringly, gazing at Heurodis's peaceful, pretty face, her creamy white silk dress, and her shining hair that lay spread out over the ground.

"Come on," said Grace, "we'll leave her to rest. I'll come and wake her later." And they soundlessly packed up the picnic and went back to the castle.

"Madam," whispered Grace gently, touching Heurodis's shoulder. "My lady. Wake up. It's late in the afternoon."

Heurodis stirred slightly, and Grace smiled. "Wake up, my lady," she said again.

But when Heurodis opened her eyes, Grace saw that she was staring wildly. Instead of looking relaxed and rested, she seemed possessed by fury.

"What do you want?" Heurodis spat suddenly, sitting up. Her eyes darted violently from side to side, and her previously smooth hair stuck out in a tangled mess, adorned with small twigs and bits of grass.

Grace put out a hand to help her up, but Heurodis clawed and scratched her with her long nails. Grace backed away in horror, clutching her bleeding hand.

"Madam?" she began, bewildered. "My lady? Are you all right—"

Then Heurodis started to scream, flailing her arms around and tearing fiercely at her own clothes and face.

Grace was horrified. Her beloved lady had obviously gone insane, somehow, here in the orchard. She should not have left her side. She ran back to the castle and got several servants, and they all carried Heurodis, screaming and struggling, back to her chamber and helped her into bed. Sir Orfeo was brought at once.

As the door closed behind him, Orfeo tentatively approached the bed where Heurodis lay. The chamber window blazed with the evening sun, making the inside of the room seem dark and gloomy. All Orfeo could see were his wife's once-beautiful eyes, staring wildly.

"My love," he said quietly. "What happened in the orchard? Do you feel ill?"

Heurodis's staring eyes became glassy with tears, which began to spill down her cheeks. Orfeo came and sat beside her, and grasped her hand. "Tell me," he whispered in her ear. "I'll help you, whatever it is."

"You. . . can't. . . help me," sobbed Heurodis in a terrified voice. "Oh Orfeo, my dear husband. . . I have to leave you," she whispered. "I *have to leave.*"

"Why?" asked Orfeo, as gently as he could. But he was worried by Heurodis's strange sickness.

"I had a dream. . ." said Heurodis, trembling. "But ~ it wasn't just a dream. It was real ~ I *know* it was real. . .

"I dreamed that I was lying in the orchard, just as I really was," Heurodis began, shivering as Orfeo wrapped his arms around her comfortingly. "My maids had gone back inside, and I was lying under the tree. Then I sat up, and suddenly I heard a quiet rustling noise. I looked down, and there I saw a snake, a small one, weaving away from me through the grass.

"But I wasn't frightened ~ it was only a little snake. I watched it go, and then I heard the sound of hooves. Suddenly, all around me, there were hundreds of knights on horseback ~ more than could possibly have fitted in the orchard. They were all around me, pressing in on me, and I thought they were going to trample on me. Their armor shone so brightly that I could hardly see.

"Then they spoke ~ it was as if they were all speaking at once, hundreds of them, but I couldn't see any one of them open his mouth. There was just this huge voice in my head, and it said: *'You must come with us!'*

"I answered them back, and said, 'No I won't! I'm not going anywhere, I'm staying here with my maids!'

"But then their king came forward. He was riding a white horse, and he had long black hair, and a crown that wasn't gold or silver, but carved out of a kind of precious stone. It shone as brightly as the sun, and almost blinded me as he came toward me.

"He was strange," said Heurodis, in a weak, quiet voice. "Attractive, beautiful even, but mysterious and frightening as well. I didn't like him.

"And then he reached out and. . . and seemed to grab me, and he said 'You're coming with me.' And before I knew what was happening I was flying through the air with him and all the knights, and we soared over the wilderness, and I saw his kingdom, and his castle, woods and rivers, dark towers, forests full of strange blooms, and. . ."

"It's all right," said Orfeo, hugging his wife tightly. "It was just a dream, don't worry, you're safe now."

"But it *wasn't* just a dream, I know it wasn't," wept Heurodis, "because then he came and put me back down in the same spot under the pear tree, and he said. . . he said I would have to come back to the same place tomorrow, alone, and they'd take me to live with them forever. And if I didn't come, they'd find me and tear me limb from limb, and I'd never escape. I know it was true," said Heurodis, breaking down in tears again. "*I have to go.*" Her shoulders heaved with sobs as the bemused Orfeo hugged her tighter than ever.

"I'm sure it was just a nightmare," he reassured her, "but whatever happens, I won't let him take you. We'll have the tree guarded. If they come, they'll have to get past the best knights in the kingdom."

Orfeo immediately sent messengers to summon all the knights in Kent to come to the castle. By the next morning, over a thousand fully armed fighters had arrived.

Orfeo went with Heurodis and her maids to the pear tree, and he arranged the knights of the kingdom around them, facing outwards, with their weapons drawn. As many as possible were crammed into the orchard. The rest were posted outside, around the old stone walls, staring at the horizon for any sign of an approaching army.

Heurodis was trembling and white with fear, but Orfeo and Grace held her hands tightly and tried to soothe her with kind words as they waited.

"Nothing to worry about," said Grace sensibly.

"No one's taking you anywhere," Orfeo reassured his wife.

But Heurodis could only glance nervously about with a blank, terrified face.

They waited. One moment, there was no sound but the sweet trilling of the birds in the orchard, Heurodis's shallow breathing, and the occasional jangle from the bridles of the knights' horses.

The next moment, the air was filled with a long, miserable scream, and Orfeo knew it was his wife's voice. "No-ooooo-oooooooo!" she cried, startling the horses, who were all poised and ready to charge. All the knights gripped their sword hilts tightly and prepared to defend their lady.

Orpheus and Grace turned to comfort Heurodis. But they saw only each other.

No army had appeared, no king had threatened them. But Heurodis had disappeared, suddenly and invisibly, and Orpheus and Grace saw, to their horror, that they were left holding each other's hands, with no one in between.

"But my lord," pleaded Merlett, "you can't just leave! You can't abandon your kingdom!"

Sir Orfeo stood before his most trusted advisers, his face wet with tears. He clutched his forehead miserably in his hands.

"I can't rule without her," he sobbed. "I can't stay in the castle we shared!"

"Maybe she'll come back. . ." offered Merlett kindly, touching Orfeo's arm. "I mean, we don't know. . ."

"She'll never come back!" Orfeo wailed, wrenching himself away and staring at the ground. "And if I can't have her, I'll never look at another woman again! Merlett," he sniffed, turning for one last look at his dear friend, "you're in charge. I'm going. And when you hear that I'm dead, elect yourselves a new leader."

And with that, Sir Orfeo stomped away down the hall and out into the sunshine, stopping only to pick up his harp, which lay idly by the doorway.

On and on Orfeo tramped, half blinded by tears, as the sun sank and darkness crept over the land, until he came to the edge of his kingdom. Beyond, as he well knew, lay the wilderness.

With a last glance over his shoulder, Orfeo crossed the boundary into that barren region of wild beasts, murderous monsters and strange magic. He didn't care if he was eaten by a lion or drowned in a swamp. He just wanted to leave, to forget Heurodis and the happiness he had lost.

But Sir Orfeo did not die. He ate berries and wild fruits, and slept on a bed of moss and leaves. When winter came, he dug up roots and collected nuts, and sheltered inside hollow trees.

He passed the time playing his harp, and instead of attacking him, the beasts of the wilderness ~ snakes, wolves, lions and lizards, and birds of the forest ~ crept closer to listen to the beautiful music.

Ten years passed by, and Orfeo lived as a wild man, wandering further and further away from his old kingdom. He had grown thin and wiry, browned by the sun and scarred and dirty from sleeping on the ground. His beard hung down to his waist, tangled with twigs and sticky bush-burrs, and his clothes were ragged and filthy.

But try as he might, he could never forget his beautiful wife Heurodis. Each and every day he mourned for her, playing sad songs on his harp as tears rolled down his dirty face.

Then, one morning, as he sat on a hillside with a lion cub curled up at his feet, Orfeo heard a strange but familiar sound.

It was a sound he hadn't heard since he left his kingdom. The sound of a hunting horn.

Now, everyone knew that people didn't go hunting in the wilderness. It was far too dangerous.

Yet there, in the river valley below him, was a handsome king, with black hair and green hunting clothes, and a strange crown that looked as if it was carved out of shining, precious stone. The king was followed by a grand hunting party of dozens of lords and servants, and a pack of baying hounds.

Orfeo stopped strumming his harp and stared. Something about the strange king seemed familiar. He got up and quietly set off down the hillside to get a better look.

But by the time he came to the riverbank, the king's party had passed by. Peeking out from behind a rowan tree, Orfeo saw instead a crowd of ladies with hunting hawks, all dressed in bright silk dresses of every shade. He gazed in astonishment at their beauty.

One lady in particular caught his eye. Her dress was long and creamy white, and it brushed the thick grass as she walked. She carried a dazzling white falcon on her wrist.

With a familiar stabbing pain in his heart, Orfeo realized why he liked this lady best. Her long, honey-brown hair, her careful step in the grass, her pale skin ~ they all reminded him of his lovely Heurodis.

Then the lady suddenly raised her head, and looked Orfeo directly in the eye, with a sad gaze of longing.

It *was* Heurodis.

Orfeo's legs went weak and he fell to his knees behind the rowan tree. He could feel his heartbeat thumping in his throat. He tried to call out, but he could only produce a strangled moan as the ladies moved away and Heurodis disappeared into the crowd.

Orfeo followed the group at a distance, stealing from one bush to another, hiding behind rocks and clumps of bracken, and when he came to a bend in the river, he saw at once where the royal party was heading.

On the horizon ahead of them, an amazing palace lit up the sky. Its outer walls were made of gleaming crystal, and a hundred turreted towers clustered inside, built of all kinds of precious stones. The roof tiles were made of pure gold, and the whole palace shone so brightly that the land around it glowed with golden light.

Into this castle went the king on horseback, followed by the hunting party, the hounds, and lastly the ladies with their hawks. Orfeo broke into a run, and reached the palace just in time to slip inside its crystal doors before they boomed shut.

Orfeo stared in amazement at the walls of gleaming purple amethyst, pink quartz, sky-blue sapphire and sea-green jade. Among the towers he saw a large hall, whose walls were pure silver. Standing before it, Orfeo caught sight of his reflection. He saw how filthy and wild he looked, with his dirty rags and matted beard. He was completely out of place. But he had to find Heurodis.

"Who are you?" demanded a squeaky voice above him. Orfeo looked up. A gnome-like porter was leaning out of a little hatch in the huge silver doors of the hall.

"I'm, er. . . a minstrel," said Orfeo, suddenly remembering his harp and waving it uncertainly at the porter. "I'd like to come

On the horizon ahead of them, an amazing palace lit up the sky.

in and entertain the king, if that would please his majesty."

"Come in," said the porter casually, and the silver doors began to swing open. Orfeo was surprised that he didn't ask any more questions, but thanked him politely. He stepped into the hall.

Sir Orfeo had been amazed enough at the king's hunting party, and at spotting Heurodis in the crowd, and at the bright light of the mysterious palace. But what he saw now was a thousand times stranger.

On every side of him, throughout the huge silver hall, Orfeo saw the huntsmen and ladies he had seen in the wilderness, and many others besides, in all kinds of odd and violent situations.

Some stood there with swords sticking right through their bodies. Others had had their arms or legs chopped off, and one even stood upright although his head lay on the floor. Some were on horseback, dressed in armor as if taking part in a battle, while others appeared to be choking on food at a dinner table, or drowning in a flood, or consumed and shrivelled up by fire. Some simply seemed to be lying asleep in bed.

Slowly, gradually, it dawned upon poor Sir Orfeo that all these people were dead. These must be the moments of all their deaths.

"Heurodis. . ." he breathed to himself, in horrible realization, with tears pricking his eyes. He had to find her ~ even if it was just to say goodbye.

He ran through the hall, looking carefully at every lady: ladies falling off cliffs, ladies being swept away by fierce currents, ladies lying thin and weak with disease.

And then, at last, Orfeo saw a familiar pear tree.

Beneath it, in her lovely white dress, with her hair spread out over the grass, lay Lady Heurodis. And coiled around her bare ankle was a tiny little snake.

"Who are YOU?"

Orfeo jumped. In front of him there were two thrones. On one of them

100

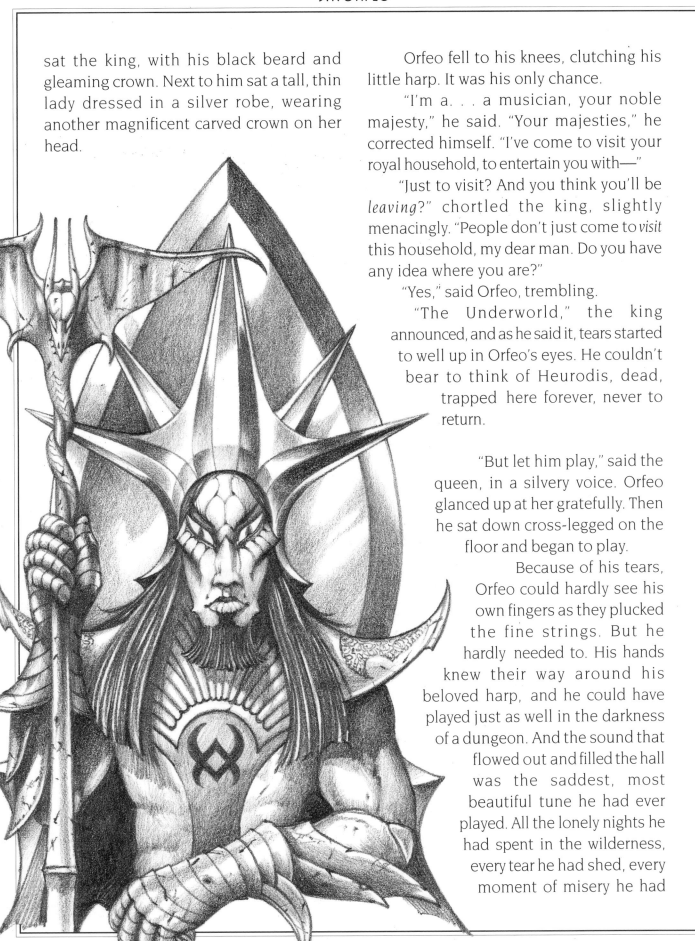

sat the king, with his black beard and gleaming crown. Next to him sat a tall, thin lady dressed in a silver robe, wearing another magnificent carved crown on her head.

Orfeo fell to his knees, clutching his little harp. It was his only chance.

"I'm a. . . a musician, your noble majesty," he said. "Your majesties," he corrected himself. "I've come to visit your royal household, to entertain you with—"

"Just to visit? And you think you'll be *leaving*?" chortled the king, slightly menacingly. "People don't just come to *visit* this household, my dear man. Do you have any idea where you are?"

"Yes," said Orfeo, trembling.

"The Underworld," the king announced, and as he said it, tears started to well up in Orfeo's eyes. He couldn't bear to think of Heurodis, dead, trapped here forever, never to return.

"But let him play," said the queen, in a silvery voice. Orfeo glanced up at her gratefully. Then he sat down cross-legged on the floor and began to play.

Because of his tears, Orfeo could hardly see his own fingers as they plucked the fine strings. But he hardly needed to. His hands knew their way around his beloved harp, and he could have played just as well in the darkness of a dungeon. And the sound that flowed out and filled the hall was the saddest, most beautiful tune he had ever played. All the lonely nights he had spent in the wilderness, every tear he had shed, every moment of misery he had endured ~ Orfeo thought of these as he plucked carefully at the strings. And each note he played spoke so clearly of his sadness that everyone in the great hall was forced to listen.

The crowds of the dead began to wander toward him as the music echoed around the silver walls and filled the air with the very essence of sorrow itself. The queen raised her hand to her mouth, her lips trembling as a tear dropped softly down her white cheek. The king looked down at his feet, and furtively wiped his eyes from time to time.

When Orfeo had finished the tune, he gave a large sniff and looked up. In front of him, among the crowds of dead men and women, he saw Heurodis, gazing at him with more beauty and longing than he could bear. He turned quickly to the king.

"I hope my music has pleased you," was all he could think of to say.

It was the queen's haunting voice that broke the silence.

"You shall have any reward you choose in return for your beautiful music," she said. At once Orfeo saw an alarmed expression cross the king's face.

"Yes, he shall," the queen repeated firmly. "Your reward, Sir?"

Almost instictively, Orfeo stepped forward and took Heurodis's hand. It was warm and soft, just as it had always been. Orfeo couldn't believe this was happening.

"I would like the Lady Heurodis as my reward," he said in a cracked whisper.

"No!" shouted the king suddenly. "You can't do this! I mean. . ." he looked at them helplessly. "You make a *terrible* couple: her so beautiful and you so shaggy and filthy.

You can't take her *back*, you can't just—"

But the queen smiled and took the king's hand calmly. "Just this once, dear," she said, with a pacifying smile. The king looked annoyed, but he said nothing.

"Orfeo," said the queen in her chilling voice. So she *did* know his name. "You are free to leave with your wife. You have proved that your love is more powerful even than. . ."

She stopped. "Go," she said simply. "Leave now. And Heurodis," she added, with a kind twinkle in her eye. Heurodis looked up.

"Watch out for snakes," the queen said.

The following evening, after walking for miles, Orfeo and Heurodis finally came within sight of the towers of their old palace. Pretending to be a poor minstrel and his wife, they begged a night's lodging from a farmer. The man looked surprised at Orfeo's rags and Heurodis's white dress, but he let them in.

The next morning Sir Orfeo set out for the palace, taking his harp but leaving Heurodis at the farm. People stared as he walked through the streets. The prosperous citizens of Kent rarely saw anyone so dirty.

But as he approached his old home, he knew he would find hospitality. At least, he would if Merlett had continued the palace's policy of welcoming all travelling musicians.

And indeed, as he reached the palace he could hear the faint strains of a fiddle playing. He smiled to himself, remembering the happy atmosphere he had once enjoyed.

"Come in, Sir!" called a uniformed guard. "I see you're a minstrel ~ and in need of a good dinner, by the look of it!" Orfeo allowed himself to be led through the grand rooms and passageways where he had once lived, until he came to the great hall. There he was given a seat at the table. At last, when he had eaten, a grey-haired old man wearing a purple robe approached him.

"Merlett!" Orfeo wanted to shout, but he stopped himself. He wanted to see if his old deputy had remained loyal to him.

"You're welcome in this house, Sir," Merlett said, sitting down opposite Orfeo. "Our only request is that you play for us. I see you're a harpist. Ah, if our Sir Orfeo were here, he'd play a merry duet with you!"

"I'd be delighted to play you a tune," said Orfeo. He picked up his grubby, worn old harp, and began to strum a happy jig. It had been one of his favorite tunes when he lived at the palace.

At first Merlett closed his eyes and listened ecstatically. Then a frown passed across his face. He opened his eyes and stared at the harp.

"I'm sorry," he interrupted. "It's just that I. . . I think I've heard that harp before. I think I've *seen* it before," he said, puzzled. "Would you mind telling me where you got it from?"

"Ah, that's easy to answer," said Orfeo cunningly. "I was wandering in the wilderness about ten years ago, when I found a deserted cave. In the cave were the remains of some unfortunate soul who'd been torn to pieces by lions. Nearby, I found this harp ~ it must have belonged to that poor man. So I kept it."

"Oh, Sir Orfeo!" wailed Merlett. "That was my beloved lord, Sir Orfeo! And this is his harp! He's dead! Oh Orfeo, I'll never see you again!" And several servants and lords rushed to Merlett's aid as he fell into a faint.

From this, Orfeo knew for certain that Merlett had waited for him faithfully. And when Merlett had come round and was being comforted by the butler, he spoke again.

"What would you say," he began carefully, "if I told you that I myself was Sir Orfeo?" Merlett and the assembled lords and servants looked at the ragged, long-bearded minstrel distrustfully.

"What would you say," Orfeo went on, "if I told you I hadn't died, but had wandered in the wilderness for ten years? And had come to a strange palace, where I found Heurodis, and won her away with my harp-playing? And had brought her back safe and sound, and left her lodging with a farmer while I came here to test your loyalty?

"What would you say, Merlett, if I had discovered ~ as I have indeed discovered ~ that you were the most loyal deputy a lord could wish for?"

Merlett stared at him with a mixture of disbelief and joy, as all the other lords, servants and musicians came crowding around the table.

Then Merlett leaped up, flung the table aside and rushed forward, throwing his arms around his dear lord and master.

Soon, Orfeo had washed and shaved and put on new clothes, Lady Heurodis had been brought from the farm, and the couple had been recrowned in a grand ceremony. And the partying, music-making and celebrating that went on that night was louder, rowdier and more prolonged than any that had been seen in Orfeo's palace before.

CHAPTER ELEVEN

SIR GAWAIN AND LADY RAGNELL

The frost on the grass sparkled in the sun as King Arthur's hunting party galloped through Inglewood Forest, on the outskirts of Carlisle. It was the day after Christmas. The weather was clear, crisp and bright, and the horses were enjoying the exercise, kicking their legs up high, with thick plumes of breath snorting from their nostrils into the cold air.

But something was wrong. Sir Kay turned his horse around suddenly.

"Where's the king?" he asked. The rest of the hunting party came to a halt. They stared at each other and into the depths of the dark forest around them.

"Don't know," said Sir Tor, as his glossy black horse ambled sideways, tossing its head. "He was beside you a few minutes ago."

At that moment, King Arthur was several miles away. He had seen the golden flanks of a fallow deer among the dark tangle of trees, and had set off in pursuit, with no time to explain. Now he was nearing the end of his chase. The deer was caught in front of a large overhanging rock surrounded by bushes, and had nowhere to turn.

Arthur slowed down and carefully reached behind him for his hunting bow. He fitted a steel-tipped arrow into the bow, silently drew back the cord, and took aim.

"Well! If it isn't King Arthur!" boomed a deep, sarcastic voice.

Arthur jumped. His fingers fumbled, the bowstring slipped, and the carefully aimed arrow twanged pathetically off to one side, bouncing against a nearby tree. The deer took its chance to escape and sprang past him, disappearing into the forest.

Arthur looked around in exasperation.

Right behind him, dressed in full armor and carrying a huge sword, was one of the biggest knights Arthur had ever seen. He was leaning calmly against a rock, and the visor of his helmet was raised, revealing an enormous, hairy face with an unpleasant sneering expression on it.

"Greetings, Sir Knight," ventured Arthur politely.

"Greetings," replied the knight. "Now get ready to die."

His hand moved casually toward the hilt of his great sword and Arthur instinctively reached for Excalibur, when he remembered that he was out hunting and hadn't brought his sword with him ~ only a small dagger. He would have to rely on his wits.

"Th-there's no need for that, surely," he blustered, as the knight began to draw the bright silver blade slowly out of its scabbard.

"What have I done to upset you?" Arthur asked, trying to delay the knight's

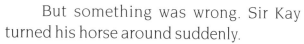

104

Right behind him was one of the biggest knights Arthur had ever seen.

actions while he thought about what to do. "Whatever it is I'm sure it can remedied."

He looked around nervously, wishing he hadn't left his knights so far behind.

"Well," said the strange knight again, freezing with his sword half-drawn, and looking into Arthur's eyes, "you've been giving away land. Land that belongs to me."

Arthur had no idea what the knight was talking about.

"In fact, I think you gave part of this forest to Sir Gawain only this year. And it wasn't yours to give."

"Excuse me," began Arthur, "but I do happen to be the King of Logres. I have—" He broke off. The knight had drawn the rest of the sword out of the scabbard, and Arthur could see how sharp it was. He tried another approach.

"It would be dishonorable to kill an unarmed man," Arthur went on quickly. "Especially the king!" he added, trying to sound lighthearted. "Look, why don't I make it up to you somehow. I'll give you whatever you ask for."

"All right then," said the knight, in his deep, velvety voice, and Arthur thought he could see the flicker of a sarcastic smile behind the thick, black beard as the stranger slid the sword back into its scabbard. "In that case, you can go on a little quest for me."

Arthur felt angry and humiliated, but there was nothing he could do. He'd promised the knight whatever he wanted.

"What quest?" he demanded.

"After a year and a day," said the knight, "come to my castle, which is near here. Dress just as you are now, and make sure you come alone. If you can answer my question, you'll be free to go. If you can't, I'll kill you."

"Very well," said Arthur, with a sigh. "And what's the question?"

"The question," said the knight with a sly smirk, "is: 'What do women want most?'"

"What a ridiculous question!" protested Arthur, who was starting to feel annoyed. He was also beginning to suspect that his sister had something to do with this. He didn't know why she would bother with this stupid riddle, but Morgan's schemes never failed to amaze him with their inventiveness.

"My name," roared the strange knight, "in case you should need to ask for me, is Sir Gromer Somer Joure. Sir Gromer Somer Joure!" He broke into a loud burst of laughter, which echoed around the gloomy forest.

Arthur had had enough. Infuriated, he spurred on his horse and galloped back the way he had come. As he went, the knight's laughter grew fainter, but Arthur couldn't stop the eerie shout of "Sir Gromer Somer Joure!" from echoing in his ears.

When Arthur met up with his men, they could see by his face that he was in an extremely bad mood. They assumed he'd had bad luck while hunting, and he certainly didn't seem to want to talk about it. It was a silent and subdued party of huntsmen that plodded back into the castle courtyard as the sun sank behind the hills.

"If you don't mind my saying so, your majesty," said Gawain tactfully, "something seems to be troubling you." Gawain hadn't been in the hunting party, but at dinner that evening he could tell that something was wrong. As Arthur's nephew, he was one of his most loyal knights and closest friends.

"Oh, Gawain," Arthur confided miserably. "I think Morgan le Fay's really got me cornered this time. I don't know what I'm going to do." And he told Gawain all about the encounter with the strange knight, who called himself Sir Gromer Somer Joure and who had asked the peculiar question, 'What do women want most?'

"Hmmm," mused Gawain. "That *is* a strange question!"

"And I've got to accept the challenge," Arthur went on, "because I promised him whatever he wanted. But I've no idea how I'm going to find the answer. I'm sure Morgan is behind this," he added, tapping the table in frustration.

Gawain frowned. "I think we can manage it," he said at last. "I'll help you. All we need to do is go to as many towns and cities as possible, and ask as many people as we can what the answer is. I'll go one way, you go another."

Arthur didn't look convinced.

"I mean, we've got a whole year," Gawain reassured him, "and we can write down all the answers, so we don't forget them. One of them's *sure* to be right."

A bright January morning a few days later found Gawain and Arthur preparing to set off. The king was too embarrassed to tell the whole court that he was going to try to find out what women wanted most, so he had simply said that he and Gawain were going on a tour of the kingdom, visiting small towns and villages that didn't usually see the king or his knights from one year to the next.

But Gawain had secretly borrowed two sheaves of parchment bound with leather, two bottles of ink and a stock of quill pens from the local monastery. When they set out in different directions from Carlisle, this equipment was stashed deep in their saddlebags.

As winter turned to spring, and all through the hot and dusty summer, the knight and the king wandered their separate ways, filling their books with people's responses to the strange question. Everyone seemed to have a different answer.

"That's easy!" roared the fat old innkeeper at the tavern where Gawain stayed on the first night. "Women want nice new bonnets. Obvious, isn't it? My wife's always hankering after a new bonnet, aren't you, my dear!" The innkeeper's wife waved cheerily from the kitchen. Gawain wasn't sure that this was the right answer for *all* women, but he dutifully took out his book and wrote it down.

"What do women want most?" pondered the Archbishop thoughtfully, as Arthur sat in his plush palace, drinking a goblet of wine before dinner. "I should think they want to meet a nice young man and settle down, most of them. Marriage, that's what women want, I'm sure of it," decided the Archbishop, taking another slurp of wine. Arthur carefully wrote the answer in his book.

"Beauty," said a father of six daughters, as he and Gawain and the other villagers watched the girls of a tiny village dancing around the maypole on a warm spring afternoon. "They just want to be beautiful, so that all the young men will look at them."

He sighed. "You're not looking for a wife, are you, by any chance?" Shaking his head apologetically, Gawain took out his pen and ink to write down the answer.

It was the middle of December when Gawain and Arthur finally met up again at the now empty castle in Carlisle. Everyone else had gone back to Camelot for that year's Christmas feast.

The two men compared their books full of answers. Every page was crammed with responses collected from all over the land. Beggars and barons, priests and peasants, squires and servants from every corner of the kingdom had offered their opinions about what women wanted most, and all of them were different.

"You see?" said Gawain cheerfully. "We've got hundreds! One of these has got to satisfy Sir Gromer Somer Joure. All we've got to do is take them along to show him, and then we can get back to Camelot just in time for New Year!"

"I don't know." Arthur looked troubled. "What if we haven't got the right answer?"

But there was nothing he could do. He had no choice but to head into Inglewood Forest and look for Sir Gromer Somer Joure's castle.

After a whole morning's riding, the two men finally came to the spot where, over a year before, Arthur had met the strange knight. They rode around the overhanging rock, and in front of them was a frost-covered meadow, leading up to a crooked castle of black stone.

"That must be it," said Arthur, with a resigned shrug. "Well, I'd better take both books. He said I had to be alone."

Gawain handed over his own book, but as he did so, he noticed a figure on a white horse coming toward them.

"Arthur!" he whispered. "Is that him?"

Arthur spun around. But the rider who approached them was not Sir Gromer Somer Joure at all. It was a lady, dressed in flowing white robes, and they could see that her horse's bridle and her cloak were decorated with precious jewels.

As she rode nearer to them, however, they also realized that she was exceptionally ugly.

In fact, she was the most hideously repulsive woman that either of them had ever laid eyes on.

Her face was red and covered with huge, weeping boils. Her nose was long, warty and pointed. Her mouth was almost as wide as her face, and a trickle of dribble ran down her hairy chin from between her black and yellow teeth. Her pale green eyes seemed to bulge right out of her head, and her filthy, louse-infested hair stuck out from under her bonnet in ugly tufts.

"Good day to you, my lady,"

said Arthur, as politely as ever, while Gawain tried very hard not to stare.

"Well, hello, King Arthur!" the lady squawked. She had an awful, high-pitched, squealing voice which made the two knights wince.

"May we help you in any way, my lady?" asked Gawain.

"More to the point," shrieked the hideous crone, pointing a long finger with a sharp fingernail at the books under Arthur's arm, "I think I can help *you*. I know what you're here for. And I'm sorry to say, not one of the answers you have written down in those books is the right one."

"Oh no," groaned Arthur, burying his face in his hands. "I knew it. I knew it."

"But," cackled the lady, "I *do* know the answer. And I'll tell you it."

Arthur looked up again at her revolting face, his heart filling with hope. This was his last and only chance of finding out what women really did want most.

"In return for a small favor, of course," she went on.

"Anything!" said Arthur, although Gawain tried to interrupt. But it was too late.

"Good!" barked the lady. "I want a husband. I'm not married yet, you see, and I'd really like to marry a Knight of the Round Table."

Gawain froze. He felt his heart sink, like a stone plunging to the bottom of a very deep and murky lake.

"Well," said Arthur, brightly. "I can't speak for myself, of course, because I'm the king, and anyway I'm married already. And ~ well, it's not for me to make a promise like that on behalf of one of my knights. I mean, I couldn't possibly do that, could I? Could I, Gawain?"

Gawain and Arthur looked at each other. Arthur glared desperately at Gawain. Gawain frowned stubbornly, trying to pretend he couldn't understand what the king meant.

"Well then!" squawked the loathsome lady, after a painfully long silence. "Have it your own way. You'll just have to die an agonizing death at the hands of Sir Gromer Somer Joure, I suppose!"

"All right!" shouted Gawain. He couldn't let Arthur die. "All right. I mean, of course, my lady. I would be honored if you would consent to be my wife."

"Jolly good!" yelped the woman, grinning a huge and disgusting grin. "Well, you come over here, your majesty, so I can whisper the answer to you."

Squirming uncomfortably, Arthur steered his horse toward the lady and leaned over to hear the answer. She whispered in his ear, spraying his cheek with slimy spit. Gawain felt sick, but Arthur suddenly seemed to have cheered up enormously.

"See you in a minute, Gawain!" he cried, galloping off toward Sir Gromer Somer Joure's castle with the two books still tucked under his arm.

Sir Gromer Somer Joure was standing on the drawbridge as Arthur approached the castle. He looked just as huge and fearsome as Arthur remembered.

"So!" roared the knight, "what have you got for me, eh?" He stepped forward and immediately wrenched the two books from under Arthur's arm.

"But, no, you don't understand," Arthur protested, trying to grab the books back from the huge knight's vice-like grasp. "You see, those aren't. . ."

"Marriage!" shouted the knight scornfully, flicking through the pages and reading out one answer after another. "Beauty! Children! Nice clothes! Ha, ha, hah! Money! Freedom from drudgery! Cake recipes! A new *bonnet*?!" He laughed uproariously at all the answers, and finally threw both books on the ground. "I'm afraid you've had it, King Arthur!" he yelled, once again grasping the hilt of his massive sword.

"Wait!" shouted Arthur. "You're not listening to me! I'll tell you what women want most. It's..."

"Yes?" enquired the knight, with a sarcastically interested expression.

"It's... it's... to have control over men," breathed Arthur at last. He hoped it really was the right answer.

He needn't have worried. A look of dread passed over Sir Gromer Somer Joure's face and he suddenly let out a long, agonized, gurgling scream.

"That evil WITCH, Lady Ragnell!" he shrieked. "She told you the answer to try to free herself. But she'll never escape! NEVER!" he howled, retreating into his dark castle. The drawbridge closed suddenly, with a bang like a thunderclap.

Trembling with relief, Arthur rode back to where Gawain and his hideous bride-to-be were waiting. He tried to greet them with a friendly smile, but Gawain looked up at him sullenly.

"Thank you," said Arthur to Lady Ragnell. "Thank you so much. You've saved my life. And," he said quietly to Gawain, "thank you too, Gawain. I really do appreciate your help."

"My pleasure," replied Gawain as politely as possible, so as not to hurt the lady's feelings.

"Well!" broke in the lady's unbearable squawking voice. "Now I'm to be married, I'd like to get to know my fiancé a little better!"

Gawain shuddered, but tried not to show it.

"You ride on ahead, King Arthur," she continued, "and make preparations for our wedding. I'll ride with Gawain!"

So, casting one last, guilty glance at Gawain, Arthur spurred his horse and set off at full speed for Camelot.

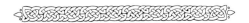

"It's him!" cried a servant girl, peering out of a window in the kitchen of Camelot. "It's Gawain and his new bride!"

As the news spread, everyone poured out of the castle to greet the happy couple. Arthur hadn't told them what Gawain's bride looked like. He had only said Gawain was getting married.

The crowd of knights, ladies, servants and townspeople waved and cheered loudly as the two figures on horseback neared the castle gates.

But when they came closer, the cheering gradually stopped. People fell silent and looked away in embarrassment and disbelief. Men frowned at each other in horror. Small boys sniggered. Girls whispered cruelly to each other that Gawain's girlfriend was an ugly old witch.

However, Gawain was a noble and chivalrous knight, and he introduced his lady to everyone as chivalrously and respectfully as if she were the most beautiful woman in the world. He tried to forget about his own feelings, and instead reminded himself that he had done this to save King Arthur's life, which was surely something he should be proud of.

The wedding ceremony was held that very day, and, leading his wife by the hand, Gawain took his place at the Round Table for the wedding feast.

Unfortunately, his bride did not have very good table manners. The other knights and ladies tried not to look as she slurped her wine, gobbled her dinner, belched loudly, and talked with her mouth full, spraying the guests with pieces of chewed food. Meanwhile, Gawain smiled as graciously as possible.

At last the feast was over. Full of fine food and wine, and tired out from talking and dancing, the knights and ladies began to depart, each stopping to wish the newlyweds good night. Gawain tried to make the farewells last as long as possible, but eventually everyone was gone from the great hall, and he had to face the unpleasant truth.

It was time to take his new wife back to his living quarters.

Up the winding stone staircases, along the narrow candlelit passages decorated with beautiful carvings, and through the hallways hung with dark tapestries, Lady Ragnell followed her new husband, puffing and panting, until they finally came to his lodgings. Gawain turned the key in the keyhole and pushed the door open, standing aside politely to let his wife through first.

"Well then," he said with some embarrassment, "welcome to your new home, my dear."

"Aren't you going to kiss me, then?" screeched his wife, leaning over to him with a wide, expectant grin. Her breath smelled disgusting.

"Erm. . . of course," said Gawain.

He took a deep breath.
He closed his eyes.
Then, trying not to feel sick, he leaned forward and planted a single kiss on Lady Ragnell's wrinkled, slobbery lips.

All of a sudden, Gawain couldn't bear it a moment longer. He let out a long, agonized moan of misery, clapped his hands over his face and threw himself face down on his bed. What had he done? How could he have married Lady Ragnell? How would he ever be able to stand it, sharing his home with this hideous hag, year after year after year? Even though he was a grown man and a brave knight, his eyes started to fill with tears at the horrible thought.

"Gawain."

It was not the familiar, unbearable squawk that called him. It was a soft, gentle voice, low and quiet.

"Gawain. Please turn around. Please look at me."

Gawain sat up on the bed. He pressed his fists into his eyes, pushing away the tears. He looked.

There, standing right in the middle of his bedchamber, was a lovely young woman with beautiful eyes and glossy, chestnut-brown hair. Her skin was soft and smooth, her smile was kind and gentle, and she wasn't dribbling.

"Who are you?" asked Gawain, astounded. "What are you doing here? Where's my wife gone?"

"I'm Lady Ragnell," said the woman, smiling at him. "I'm your wife."

"Really?" Gawain couldn't believe it. He reached out and took her hand. "Is it really you?"

"It's *really* me," she laughed. "This is what I really look like. Morgan le Fay put a spell on me to make me look ugly. And you broke it, by kissing me. Not many knights would have been brave enough to do that, Gawain."

"I suppose not," said Gawain, starting to laugh when he remembered the repulsive creature he had just kissed. But he still couldn't really believe his luck.

"Do you really mean," he asked her, "that that hideous old hag won't be coming back? I'll never have to see her again?"

Lady Ragnell looked troubled. She frowned and sat down on the bed.

"Well, not exactly," she said. "The thing is, the spell isn't completely broken. This is the real me, but I'll still have to be hideous for half the time ~ for twelve hours out of every twenty-four."

"Oh," said Gawain, feeling rather disappointed. Still, it was better than nothing. He took his wife's hand and squeezed it affectionately, looking into her beautiful eyes. "That's all right," he told her kindly. "I don't mind."

"But you do get to choose," added Lady Ragnell. "You can decide whether I'm ugly during the daytime, or during the night. If it's by day, of course, you'll have everyone pitying you and you'll be ashamed of me. But if it's at night, well, I'll be hideous when we're alone together . . ."

Gawain thought about it. It would be wonderful if everyone could see how beautiful his bride really was. They would congratulate him and say he was the luckiest man alive.

But on the other hand, if he chose, he could have his beautiful wife all to himself. After all, could he really bear to be alone every night with the screeching, drooling, ugly Lady Ragnell?

What must it be like for her to be stuck inside that ugly body, Gawain wondered? It must be miserable.

Eventually he said, "It's your choice."
"What?"

"I think you should choose," Gawain repeated. "You're the one who has to suffer the most. Which would you prefer ~ day or night?"

"Oh, Gawain!" cried Lady Ragnell, her eyes brimming with tears of joy. "You *are* the perfect husband after all!" She threw her arms around him and hugged him tightly, then kissed him again. Gawain looked bewildered.

"Don't you see?" she said, holding both his hands. "That was the right answer! You asked me what I wanted ~ you handed control over to me. And by doing that, you've broken the spell completely!"

"No more hideous Lady Ragnell?" Gawain asked nervously.

"Never! Never again!" she shouted exultantly, and, pulling Gawain up from the bed, his new wife danced with him around the room, singing for joy.

CHAPTER TWELVE

THE ADVENTURES OF SIR LANCELOT

There had been no battles in the Kingdom of Logres for months. There hadn't even been any decent adventures. Most of the knights were just hanging around at Camelot, jousting and holding parties. Eventually, Sir Lancelot decided it was time for him to go on a quest.

It wasn't just boredom and a desire for adventure that spurred him to leave. In fact, the opposite was true. He was enjoying being at Camelot just a little *too* much. For the longer he stayed, the more time he found himself spending with the queen.

And the longer he spent with her, the more they liked each other. Lancelot knew he must never betray Arthur, his friend and king, but he couldn't help his feelings for Guinevere. And people were already starting to gossip. The only thing to do was to make his farewells and spend some time traveling, in the hope that his love would fade.

Lancelot had only been riding for two days when he came to a strange little town. It was built of black stone, on the side of a rocky mountain, and the sunlight never seemed to penetrate its dark, narrow streets. At the top of the town, a spindly tower loomed above the houses, casting a menacing shadow.

Lancelot found an inn to stay at, and when he revealed his name, the innkeeper seemed overjoyed.

"At last!" he cried, and before Lancelot had even had time to unlace his boots or order some supper, his host had summoned the mayor, the priest and half the townspeople to the inn. They crowded around the doorway, shuffling and peering, until Lancelot felt he had better go and say hello.

A huge cheer greeted him when he stuck his head out into the street.

"Sir Lancelot," beamed the mayor, shaking him by the hand. "Welcome to our humble town! We've waited so long for a Knight of the Round Table to come and rescue our lady, who lies in agony at the top of the Tortuous Tower."

Lancelot looked up at the eerie tower, black against the evening sky, and saw that right at the top there was a tiny window, with a faint light glowing in it.

"She can't escape," added the priest. "Morgan le Fay bewitched her, because she was jealous of her beauty."

"And now she has to lie in agony, in a boiling, burning bath, all day and all night," said the innkeeper, "and only a true Knight of the Round Table can save her."

The townspeople stared expectantly at Sir Lancelot. He had obviously found the first adventure of his quest.

"I'll fetch my sword," he said.

Night was falling as Lancelot climbed the cobbled hill to the Tortuous Tower, surrounded by eager citizens. The mayor showed him the entrance, which was sealed with heavy iron bars, twisted and bound in magical knots. Lancelot recognized the work of the evil sorceress, Arthur's half-sister, and murmured a secret prayer that Merlin had taught the knights to protect them from Morgan le Fay's spells.

Then he told the people to stand back, and charged at the door. His mighty strength was enough to smash the hinges, and he stepped through into the darkness.

Inside the tower, it was as hot as an oven. The air was dank and wet and smelled of mildew. Lancelot began to feel his way upward, along the dripping walls of

the spiral staircase, his armor and sword clanking against the slippery steps. He could feel slimy

worms being squashed under his feet, and hear the rats scuttling into the corners.

As he climbed higher, the tower became narrower and narrower, until there was hardly any space to stand up. Sweating in the heat, Lancelot found himself in front of a little door, with steam billowing from its keyhole and water running down its wooden planks.

With little effort, he pushed the door down, and was immediately engulfed in hot steam.

"Where are you?" he cried.

"Here!" answered a faint voice.

Shielding his face, Lancelot pressed on into the room. Through the clouds of steam he could make out a tub of boiling, bubbling water, and in it lay a lady, moaning painfully. He could see that she was beautiful, but her face was red from the sweltering heat, and she was weak and helpless.

Lancelot reached into the boiling water, in all his armor, and lifted the lady out as quickly as possible. Then he carried her through the little doorway, stumbled over to the staircase and half ran, half slithered down the slimy steps, the lady's soaking clothes clinging to his silver armor, until at last he burst out into the cool night to the cheers of the waiting crowd.

The next morning, when Sir Lancelot was ready to go on his way, the mayor came to thank him for his bravery. Lancelot bowed modestly.

"But now, I'm afraid I must be on my way," he said, saddling his horse in the courtyard. "It has been my pleasure to stay in your delightful town."

In fact, he thought the town was spooky, but Lancelot was always polite.

"Well. . . actually," said the mayor, looking slightly awkward, "I've come to see you to ask you another favor."

Lancelot sighed to himself. Was he ever going to get away from this place?

"As a Knight of the Round Table, I am at your service," he announced graciously.

"What would you like me to do?"

"Well, you see, it's the dragon," said the mayor sheepishly. "An old prophecy says that whoever rescues our lady from the tower will also kill the terrible dragon that has terrorized our town for many centuries."

Lancelot looked around. "I must say," he began, just a little sarcastically, "I hadn't noticed a dragon."

"No, well, no, it does only come out at weekends," admitted the mayor. "Please, Sir Lancelot. We're relying on you."

So, instead of riding on his way, Sir Lancelot found himself heading even farther up the mountain, toward the cave where the townspeople had said the dragon lived.

Lancelot stopped outside the cave. He couldn't see a dragon, so he climbed down from his horse and went to investigate, drawing his sword just in case.

The sun was shining now, and butterflies darted in and out among the boulders that surrounded the cave. Lancelot shaded his eyes, trying to peer into the gloom. Then he noticed something carved on a rock right in front of the cave entrance.

Here shall come a noble knight,
To slay the dragon with courage and might;
And he shall. . .

Suddenly Lancelot stopped. He could hear breathing.

Slowly, without making any sudden movements, he looked up.

There, creeping out of the darkness of the cave, came the ugliest, slimiest, most repulsive creature Lancelot had ever seen. It was skinny and writhing, with long, jagged claws, a scaly body, and two leathery wings. Its head lolled on one side, its eyes sticking out hideously. From its nostrils came a swirl of greenish smoke that smelled disgusting.

But the whole dragon was only about the size of Lancelot himself. He couldn't believe this puny monster had been any trouble at all. Anyone could have killed it.

And without stopping to think, Lancelot leaped forward, wielding his sword, and sliced off the dragon's head. It fell onto the ground with a squelch, spilling thick, slimy green blood all over the grass.

"Now then," said Lancelot to himself, "back to that inscription."

Here shall come a noble knight,
To slay the dragon with courage and might;
And he shall leave his wife and child
To wander alone in the wilderness wild.

Lancelot looked at the sword in his hand, stained with the green blood. Then he turned around and looked at the dragon lying dead on the ground.

The inscription didn't make sense. He was only on a short trip, after all, and he didn't have either a wife or a child. In fact, it was probably about time he went back to Camelot.

He put the inscription out of his mind, wiped the sword on the grass, replaced it in its scabbard, and untied his horse.

But try as he might, Lancelot could not find the strange town where he had rescued the burning lady. He rode right around the mountain, scanning the horizon for the Tortuous Tower, but there was no sign of it.

And when he came down from the rugged slopes, he didn't recognize his surroundings at all. There were stunted, tangled trees and gnarled crags, and a chilling wind whistled across the barren landscape. Far off to one side, he could see the sea, and a black, threatening river winding its way toward it.

Then Lancelot realized. He must be in the wilderness.

The only building he could see was a ruined castle on top of a huge rock, all blackened and crumbling as if it had been hit by lightning.

When he rode around the ruin, though, he saw that part of it was still standing. He tied his horse up and went to explore, clambering over the piles of rubble until he came to the doorway of a large room that was mostly still intact.

"Hello-o-o!" called Sir Lancelot, his voice echoing through the ruins.

"Welcome!" called a weak voice.

Lancelot jumped. He hadn't expected to find anyone. He stepped through the door.

In the middle of the room was a big dining table, laid with a rich feast. Knights and ladies sat around the table. Servants brought them wine. And in the corner, lying on a beautiful velvet couch, with a huge bandage around his chest, lay a frail king, wearing a golden crown.

"Welcome to Castle Carbonek," said the king. "I am King Pelles. And you are?"

"Sir Lancelot, your majesty," said

Lancelot quickly. King Pelles smiled knowingly. "Take your place at the feast, Sir Lancelot," was all he would say. And when Lancelot looked, he saw that there was an empty chair at the table, next to a beautiful young woman. He sat down.

Lancelot only meant to stay at the castle long enough to have a rest and work out how to get back to Camelot. But whenever he spoke about leaving, King Pelles and his daughter wouldn't hear of it, and insisted he stay longer. When he asked them which was the quickest way back to Camelot, they just changed the subject.

He even secretly searched in the castle library for a map which might show him where he was, but to no avail.

The truth was, Princess Elaine, King Pelles's daughter, had fallen hopelessly in love with Sir Lancelot the minute he had first sat beside her at the feast. He was so tall and handsome, so charming and witty, that Elaine's heart started thumping whenever he came near her.

She had tried following the knight around, wearing her prettiest dresses and giggling as sweetly as possible, but Lancelot never seemed interested in her. Little did she know that he spent every spare moment dreaming of his beloved Guinevere.

Eventually, Elaine went to see her father in despair.

"He's *so* handsome," she sighed, "but he hardly ever looks at me! Surely I'd make a good wife for him ~ me, a princess! Oh, *how* can I make him love me?"

King Pelles smiled again, and a cunning look passed across his face. The old king had not forgotten how, long ago, a knight from Camelot ~ Sir Balyn was his name, Pelles remembered ~ had destroyed his castle and wounded him so badly that he had never recovered.

How could he forget? He spent every day in agony, lying on his couch wrapped in bandages. And now he saw his chance for the Round Table to repay him. If he could get Sir Lancelot to marry Elaine, and prevent him from returning home, Camelot's best knight would become Pelles's servant forever.

He turned to his daughter. "I've been thinking just what you've been thinking, my dear," he said. "Lancelot would be the perfect husband for you. And as it happens, I know of an ancient prophecy. . . now then, what did it say again. . . ?"

"Oh, *tell* me," begged Elaine.

"Ah yes, that was it," Pelles went on. "It said that one day, Carbonek and Camelot would be united by a wonderful marriage."

"*Really*!?" gasped Elaine. "You mean it's meant to be! Lancelot will be mine!"

"But it's not going to be easy," said King Pelles quickly. "Lancelot ~ well, his mind is on other things. He's going to need some encouragement. In fact, if we're going to find you a husband, we might require a little assistance."

"Well then," said Elaine briskly, "it's just as well we have Lady Brusen here to help us, isn't it? I'll go and see her this minute." And off she went.

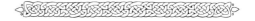

Lady Brusen was no ordinary lady-in-waiting. Her best friend was none other than Morgan le Fay, King Arthur's evil half-sister. And it was Morgan herself, of course, who had led Lancelot astray into the wilderness, where he had lost his way. Morgan le Fay knew that without his best knight, Arthur would find it much harder to defend Camelot against her wicked plans.

Morgan was still the wickedest, wiliest witch in the land, but she had taught many of her spells, charms and secret recipes to Lady Brusen. And as soon as Elaine had explained the situation to her, Lady Brusen came up with a very cunning plan.

That evening, Lancelot was sitting in the rubble-filled garden when a messenger came hurrying up to him. "A letter from my lady the queen," he panted, thrusting forward a sealed roll of parchment. Lancelot grabbed it and ripped it open. He immediately recognized Guinevere's handwriting:

My dearest Lancelot,

I have received word that you are at Castle Carbonek, and I can bear to live without you no longer. I have left Arthur. Please meet me at Castle Case tonight.

Your ever-adoring

Guinevere x x x

Lancelot was distraught. Guinevere had left Arthur? He paced agitatedly around the overgrown garden. Surely she would *never* leave him.

He read the letter again. He didn't even know where Castle Case was.

"Lancelot ~ is everything all right?" asked a kind, matronly voice. It was Lady Brusen.

"Er, well," he said, flustered, stuffing the parchment into his pocket and trying to appear calm. "Yes, everything's fine. I just. . . I wondered if you knew where Castle Case was? Is it near here?"

"Castle Case? Yes, of course, it's only five miles away," said Lady Brusen cheerily. "Fancy a spot of sightseeing, do you, Lancelot? Well, why don't we go together? I quite feel like a ride." And before Lancelot could argue, he found himself trotting through the forest next to Lady Brusen, wondering how to explain that he was going to meet Guinevere.

They soon came to a white castle set deep among trees and thorny rose bushes.

"I'd, er, hate to tire you out, my lady," began Lancelot politely. "Would you like to wait here while I go for a little walk?"

"What nonsense!" chuckled Brusen, climbing down from her horse, and smiling slyly to herself. "We can't come all this way without going inside to look around!" And she bustled off toward the gates.

Lancelot tied up the horses and followed anxiously.

"Now then," said Lady Brusen, after the porter had let them in. She was rummaging about in a cupboard, among a pile of old bottles and rusty goblets.

"Don't worry, my dear," she reassured Lancelot, who was staring nervously. "Castle Case belongs to King Pelles. And I'm sure he keeps a nice bottle of mead in here for thirsty visitors. Ah, here we are."

She poured a large cup of revolting-looking brown liquid, and handed it to him. "Go on!" she ordered him. "Drink up!"

So Lancelot took a sip. The drink was sweet and sticky. He had some more.

Then he began to feel very strange.

"This way!" called Lady Brusen merrily, dragging the dizzy knight along a passage toward a large oak door. She opened the door

and gave Lancelot a shove. He stumbled through, still clutching his goblet, and heard a bang as the door closed behind him.

"Lancelot."

Lancelot's heart jumped up into his throat at the beautiful, beloved sound of Guinevere's voice. But the room was dark.

"Where are you?" Lancelot mumbled. His speech was slow and confused, and he couldn't think properly. All he wanted was to find her.

"Here," she said, and at once he felt Guinevere's arms wrapping around him. He

hugged and kissed her in the darkness.

"What's. . . What's going on?" Sir Lancelot slurred. "Why are you here?"

"To marry you," said Guinevere's voice, sweetly. "It's all over between me and Arthur. Oh Lancelot, my love, *say* you will."

"But. . ." Lancelot protested. It didn't make sense. Guinevere would never leave Arthur ~ he knew that. But here she was. He wanted to ask her what had happened. But he felt so tired, so dizzy. . .

"Look," said Guinevere. "Here's the priest." Suddenly Lancelot saw a candle glowing in the distance. As it came closer he saw that it was carried by a figure dressed in a black robe, with a heavy hood. The next thing he knew, the priest was reciting the marriage prayers, and asking them if they would take each other as husband and wife. Guinevere's voice echoed around the room: "I do."

"I do," mumbled Sir Lancelot.

Lancelot woke up in a strange bed in an unfamiliar room. A shaft of sunlight was falling across his pillow. He rolled over. And there beside him, he saw a familiar face.

Elaine.

He had been tricked.

Lancelot began to panic as the events of the night before gradually came back to him. He had *known* there was something wrong. Guinevere ~ how he wished she was there to comfort him ~ Guinevere would never be so stupid as to leave Arthur and come and marry Lancelot in a strange castle in the forest. Why had he believed it?

And then he remembered the drink he had been given. It must have been drugged to make him so forgetful and stupid.

And stupid he had been, thought Sir Lancelot wretchedly, groaning and burying his head in the pillow. He had allowed himself, a great and noble knight, to be fooled. He had gone and married Elaine, whom he didn't even like.

But worst of all. . . Lancelot cringed at the thought.

Most terrible, embarrassing and shameful of all, he had *believed* it was Guinevere last night. And instead of saying no, as a true knight should, he had agreed to marry her. He had betrayed King Arthur.

Lancelot couldn't bear to think of it. His career was finished. How could he ever look Arthur in the eye again? He could never return to Camelot ~ but that meant. . .

He scrubbed a tear away from his eye with his fist. That meant he would never, ever see Guinevere, the woman he loved, again.

He looked helplessly at Elaine, sleeping soundly beside him. He was sure there was a smug expression on her girlish, self-satisfied face. He hated her. He didn't care if she *was* his wife ~ he could never stay with her after what she had done. There was only one thing to do. He would have to run away.

Without stopping to think for another second, Sir Lancelot, clutching his head in shame and agony, leaped out of the bed. He awkwardly pulled on his clothes, tears streaming down his face. He rushed to the window, climbed out over the stone sill, dropped down into the thorny bushes below, and ran out into the wilderness.

CHAPTER THIRTEEN

THE SEARCH FOR SIR LANCELOT

"I really don't want to alarm anyone," said Sir Gawain one evening, as the knights sat at the Round Table after supper, "but I'm a little worried about what might have happened to Sir Lancelot. I mean, it's been over a year since he left."

There was an awkward silence.

"Don't you remember?" Gawain went on. "He just took off one day, saying he was going on an adventure. He even said he wouldn't be away long. So where is he?"

Arthur began to shift about uncomfortably in his chair. Guinevere stared at the table.

It wasn't that the knights didn't *remember*. In fact, everyone at Camelot had been secretly worrying for months about where Sir Lancelot could be. But nobody had dared to say anything, because they didn't want to upset the king.

The truth was, ever since Lancelot's departure, Queen Guinevere had been heartbroken. She rarely left her chamber, and when she did, she moped miserably, wandering through the stables where Lancelot used to keep his horse, or gazing gloomily out at the horizon from one of Camelot's tallest towers.

Not surprisingly, no one wanted to mention the missing knight's name. In the end, only Gawain, Arthur's own nephew, was

brave enough to raise the matter.

"You're right, Gawain," said Arthur at last, and everyone breathed a sigh of relief. "It's high time we sent someone to search for him." He looked around the great hall.

Sir Bors pushed back his chair and stood up. He was Sir Lancelot's nephew, a big, brave and noble young knight, known for his kind heart and gentle nature.

"Your majesty," he announced. "I would be honored to undertake this quest."

"And I," put in Sir Percival from the other side of the table, "humbly beg to assist you." He stood up to face Sir Bors.

"Thank you, that's quite enough," Arthur interrupted grumpily. "I don't want to lose any more of my best knights. Sir Bors, you go east. Percival, go west. Oh, and. . . good luck."

Then the king gathered his robes about him, stood up, and silently left the hall.

That very day, Bors packed his saddlebags, chose his strongest horse, and set off. He wandered through the kingdom, and everywhere he went he asked about Sir Lancelot.

Of course, everyone had heard of the famous knight ~ but nobody said they had seen him at all in recent months. Time after time, Sir Bors was answered with blank stares, head-shaking and puzzled expressions, until he concluded that Lancelot was not anywhere to be found in the whole Kingdom of Logres.

So when, one warm and sunny day, Bors came to the edge of the kingdom, and stared ahead of him across the dark, dangerous wilderness, Bors did not stop his search. He felt something calling him, urging him onward into that unknown region, where giants lived and dragons lurked. Something in his bones told him

that this was where he might find out what had happened to his uncle. He galloped onward.

As night fell, Bors began to look around for a place to sleep. Up ahead of him he was sure he could see some kind of ruined castle through the dusk, perched on top of a steep, rocky hill. He rode nearer, and thought he could see the friendly glow of lighted windows and fires burning.

"Halt! Sir Knight!"

Bors almost jumped out of his saddle at the booming voice, which seemed to come from nowhere. Then he saw a knight dressed in black armor emerging from the shadows, mounted on a pitch-black horse.

"Prepare for battle, you cowardly cur!" shouted the knight.

"What battle?" said Bors. "And I'm not a coward! I was going to ask for a night's lodging, if that's all right with you."

"From which castle do you come?" challenged the knight pompously.

"From Camelot, actually," said Sir Bors, "and I'm a Knight of the Round Table, so if you wouldn't mind—"

"Hah! I knew it!" screamed the knight excitedly. "Sir Lancelot, my arch-enemy! Prepare to meet your doom!" And he backed up his horse, raised his lance and rushed at Sir Bors.

"I'm not Sir Lancelot!" Bors yelled, but the knight took no notice. So Bors quickly grabbed his own lance, and the two knights crashed together. Both were flung to the ground and got up, drawing their swords.

"This is stupid," panted Sir Bors, as their weapons clashed and clanged. "It's far too dark to fight. I'll beat you anyway. And I am *not* Sir Lancelot," he added, pinning his opponent up against a tree, expertly kicking the sword from his fist and holding his own blade to the other man's throat. "I'm Sir Bors, and I come in peace. So please calm down and tell me who you are."

"All right, I surrender," said the knight sulkily. Bors let him go.

"My name is Sir Bromell," the knight explained, "and I'm in love with the lady of this castle. But *she* likes Sir Lancelot. If I can only beat him in battle, she might fall in love with me instead.

"Trouble is," Sir Bromell added, frowning, "no one knows where he is."

Bors couldn't help smiling. If he could beat Sir Bromell so easily, Lancelot would have no problem.

"Sir Bromell! What are you doing?" A female voice wafted toward them from the castle, and Bors saw a beautiful lady striding through the grass. "I'm so sorry," she said to Sir Bors. "He does this to everyone. Do come in. I'm Princess Elaine, and this is Castle Carbonek."

As soon as Bors had been welcomed inside and had eaten a hearty dinner, Elaine introduced him to her father, King Pelles, a frail old man with a bandage around his chest, and her little son, Galahad, who looked strangely familiar. Bors thought it was all very odd, but he politely explained his quest and asked them when they had last seen Sir Lancelot.

Elaine suddenly went quiet, and King Pelles looked troubled.

"Well. . . he did pass this way," said Pelles carefully, glaring at his daughter. "About two years ago now. Then he. . . well, he took a funny turn. Ran off into the wilderness all of a sudden and disappeared. To be honest, he went slightly insane. And that's the last we saw of him."

"But. . . does that mean he's still out there, wandering in the wilderness?" Bors asked in horror. "I must go and look for him at once!"

"You won't find him," said Pelles sternly. "He's been gone for months now. It would be far better for you to go straight back to Camelot and tell King Arthur that Lancelot is lost forever."

"Yes," Elaine added hurriedly. "Of course, if he does turn up here again, we'll send a message to Camelot at once."

"Absolutely," put in King Pelles.

Bors eyed the old king and his daughter suspiciously, wondering again who the blond child in Elaine's arms reminded him of. He didn't know why, but it was obvious they didn't want him to find Lancelot.

"You're right," said Bors at last. "I'll set off for Camelot tomorrow."

The following morning Bors left, taking the road he had come by, as if he really was heading back to Camelot. But he could not bring himself to abandon his search for Sir Lancelot.

For many winters and summers, he wandered throughout the islands of Britain, encountering many strange adventures,

although he never did find his uncle. It was to be almost fifteen years before he would come home to Camelot.

And by then, the forces that threatened to destroy the brotherhood of the Round Table would have gathered strength. Sir Bors could never have foreseen what would happen after his return.

Sir Percival was still a young knight, and although he was brave, he was not very wise. He was always doing his utmost to prove to the other knights how bold and fearless he was.

After all, he'd once been a simple country boy, dreaming of adventures and battles. He'd won his place at the Round Table by going on a quest for Arthur, but he was still worried that people didn't think he was very brave.

So it was no surprise that when Percival left Camelot to search for Sir Lancelot, he hadn't been traveling for more than a few hours before he got himself into a fight.

His opponent was not a monstrous dragon, a terrifying giant, or even a bold warrior, but simply another wandering knight who had accidentally bumped into Sir Percival in the forest. Percival hotheadedly swore to do battle with him, even though the knight had a broken shield and a very old helmet with rust-holes in it.

"If you insist," said the stranger, and they immediately galloped toward each other on their horses. Percival was promptly knocked to the ground.

"Draw your sword," Percival shouted

boldly, picking himself up, "and dismount from your horse at once! Come on! Fight like a man!"

So the rusty-helmeted knight hopped down from his horse and drew out a long, rusty sword. The two knights began to duel, but to Percival's surprise he could not outwit his enemy.

Every time he tried to slash or stab the knight with his sword, his opponent would cunningly deflect it with his rust-spotted blade, and soon Percival had several painful cuts and bruises.

"You don't really want to fight me any more, do you?" asked the knight kindly, as Percival staggered across the grass, bleeding profusely from his wounds.

"To the death!" Percival gasped, drunk on his own bravery.

"Look, I'll give you one last chance," warned the stranger. "Surrender now, or you'll die. And that would be a waste of a fine young fighter, wouldn't it? I'm sure

126

you've got better things to do!"

Then Percival suddenly remembered his mission ~ to find Sir Lancelot.

"All right," he whispered, wincing in pain, "I give up." He sank down onto the grass, and the stranger, seeing that Percival was badly hurt, rushed to his side.

"Who. . . who are you, anyway?" said Percival, writhing on the ground. The injuries from the rusty sword were agonizing.

"My name is Sir Hector," said the knight, taking off his helmet to reveal a handsome face, with dark hair and smiling eyes. Percival wondered if he'd seen that face somewhere before.

"I'm a Knight of the Round Table," Sir Hector added, by way of explanation.

"Really?" choked Percival, feeling extremely foolish. "So am I. But I haven't met you before. . . have I?"

"No, I don't think so," said Sir Hector. "You look like young blood to me. No, it's years and years since I've been back to Camelot. I fell out with my brother, you see, a long time ago. I've often wondered how he's been getting on."

"What's his name?" asked Percival. He tried to sit up, but fell back on the grass.

"Sir Lancelot," said Hector. "Look, I really think we'd better get you to an inn or something. You don't look too well."

"Oh no," groaned Percival, feeling like a complete idiot. "I've made the most terrible mistake ~ we should have been. . . f-f-friends, not enemies." He clenched his jaw in agony. "Sir Hector, I am Sir Percival, your faithful servant. I'm on a quest to find

your brother right now, but. . . but I don't think I'm going to make it."

Percival was already so weak from loss of blood that he couldn't stand up. Hector tried to drag him across the grass toward the nearest track through the forest, hoping that someone might be passing by. But Percival screamed in pain, and Hector realized that he was about to die. He quickly kneeled down and held the young knight in his arms, whispering all the prayers he could think of and weeping with regret at what had happened.

"Tell. . . Arthur I am his. . . his loyal servant," Percival groaned weakly, his eyes rolling about in his head and his limbs twitching horribly.

Hector closed his eyes, squeezing out tears which plopped onto Percival's armor. He couldn't bear to see the young man take his final breath.

Just then, Hector became aware of a rustling sound in the woods behind him, and turned his head. He was just in time to see the corner of a purple cloak swirling behind a tree, and he thought he heard a low muttering sound. Then, nothing.

He looked back down at the wounded man in his arms.

"Hector?" groaned Percival groggily.

"Are you all right?" asked Hector. "I thought you were done for."

"Was that Merlin?" Percival said confusedly. "I thought I saw him."

"Merlin?" said Hector. It had been so long since he'd been at the Round Table, he had almost forgotten about the old magician who advised Arthur and his knights. Now he remembered the deep purple of the wizard's cloak, and his quiet, mysterious ways.

"I think he arrived just in time," said Hector. "He saved your life. I think he must want us to find Sir Lancelot."

And he helped Percival to his feet and led him through the forest until they came to an abbey, where the younger knight could rest and recover.

For many a long year, just like Sir Bors, Sir Percival and Sir Hector searched for Sir Lancelot together, with little luck. They journeyed up and down the length of the land, visiting every village and every farm, every city and every remote castle, hoping that somewhere they might at last see the missing knight.

Meanwhile, Lancelot wandered on through the wilderness.

He looked terrible. His old clothes, once expensive and glamorous, were now dirty, ragged and tattered. He was as skinny as a rake, and his haunted eyes, once so bright and handsome, stared wildly. He lived like a wild animal, eating berries and bark, drinking from streams, and sleeping in gloomy caves and hollow trees.

But even during the worst winters, when the wind chilled his bones and the icicles hung from the gnarled branches, Lancelot would not think of returning to Camelot. He was far too ashamed.

"Oh my king, noble Arthur, how could you ever forgive me?" he would wail to himself, wandering pathetically through the twisted trees. "Guinevere, my love, will I ever see you again?"

For Lancelot had married Elaine, the daughter of King Pelles, thinking that she was Guinevere. And although she wasn't really the queen, but had been disguised by magic, Lancelot knew that by agreeing to marry her, he had betrayed King Arthur. He could never forgive himself.

So he had resolved to spend the rest of his days in the farthest reaches of the wilderness, cold and alone, as a punishment for his terrible crime.

In fact, King Pelles had been right. Sir Lancelot, renowned as the bravest, wittiest and most charming of all the Knights of the Round Table, was no longer the man he had once been. The terrible shame, guilt and sorrow he had suffered had driven him insane. And with every day that passed, he grew thinner, weaker and closer to death.

One hot summer's morning at Castle Carbonek, Princess Elaine decided to go for a walk. She sighed as she strolled over the straggly grass.

She was happy enough with her life, she thought to herself. Her son, Galahad, was her pride and joy ~ he was growing up so strong and handsome, and doing so well at the remote abbey where she had sent him to learn to read, write and behave like a brave and chivalrous knight.

But Elaine often though of her long-lost

husband, Sir Lancelot, and wished things had turned out differently. It had now been over ten years since, with the help of her maid, Lady Brusen, Elaine had tricked Lancelot into marrying her. And the very next day, as soon as he'd realized what had happened, Lancelot had disappeared.

Elaine sighed again. How handsome and charming he'd been! Every time she looked at Galahad she was reminded of Lancelot's good looks.

As she daydreamed her way across the fields near the castle, Elaine tripped over something long and heavy lying in the grass.

It was a man. A tall, emaciated and extremely dirty man, who seemed to have collapsed face-down in the meadow from exhaustion.

"Ugh!" shrieked Elaine, thinking it must be a tramp. She ran off to get Lady Brusen, and the two women carefully pushed the body over onto its back, using their toes. But then Elaine sank to her knees in amazement and shock.

"Lancelot!" she whispered, her eyes full of tears. "He's come back to me!"

"Come back for a decent dinner, more like!" muttered Lady Brusen under her breath. "He's all skin and bones!"

But however much she kissed him and shook him and slapped his face, Elaine couldn't wake the handsome knight. He was breathing, but he was clearly very ill, and Elaine was terrified he would die. She begged Lady Brusen to heal him with magic, but Brusen refused.

"He's too far gone for that," she said.

"Carry him into the chapel. He'll have to take his chance."

So Elaine called her manservants to carry Lancelot into the crumbling old chapel of Castle Carbonek, where they laid him down in front of the altar. Still weeping, Elaine lit candles to surround the sleeping knight, and kneeled down beside him. She stayed there for the whole night, praying that he would recover.

At last, slowly and sleepily, Lancelot's brown eyes opened.

"Lancelot," Elaine murmured, as alluringly as possible. "It's me, Elaine. Your wife."

Lancelot hadn't meant to return to Elaine. It was purely by chance that he'd stumbled, half dead from starvation, toward Castle Carbonek.

But even though she had saved his life, Lancelot groaned to himself when he saw Elaine. Although he blamed himself for his weakness and foolishness, he hadn't forgiven Elaine for tricking him, and he did not love her at all.

He decided it must be his destined punishment to spend his days with a wife he didn't love, and never to see Guinevere again. And he could hardly refuse when Elaine took him in, fed him, gave him new clothes, and begged him to stay. After all, she had saved his life. So he lived with her for several months, and spent every day secretly dreaming of Guinevere.

However, now that he was his old self again, Lancelot was bored. He didn't like being with Elaine, he longed for his beloved friends, and he missed his old life of jousting and questing.

So when, one day, he heard that a big tournament was to take place at the Joyous Isle, near Castle Carbonek, Sir Lancelot couldn't resist taking part.

Secretly, he sent a dwarf to the tournament to announce that "The Trespassing Knight" would soon be arriving. Then, making sure Elaine was out riding, he dressed up in black armor from head to toe, and set off for the Joyous Isle on the blackest horse he could find in the stables.

Not surprisingly, Lancelot won every joust he took part in. Although he was out of practice, he was still the cleverest, boldest and most skillful knight in the world.

No one guessed who the mysterious Trespassing Knight really was, because Lancelot never took off his black helmet. He was still too ashamed of himself to reveal his identity.

But by the end of the afternoon, he had beaten all the other knights there, and was about to be named champion of the tournament.

The lord of the Joyous Isle stepped forward, clutching a gleaming medal.

"Well, I think I speak for all of us here today," he announced, "when I say that this has been one of the most exciting tournaments we've had at the Joyous Isle for many a long year!" The crowd cheered.

"The Trespassing Knight has entertained us all with his amazing skill and bravery," the lord continued, "and we congratulate him on being—"

"Latecomers!" yelled the gatekeeper, rudely interrupting the lord's speech. Two tired-looking knights were being ushered over the drawbridge.

"Ah, well, we can't name a champion, of course, until every knight has fought," said the lord. "Ladies and gentlemen, it seems the show is not over yet!"

Lancelot won his joust with the first knight easily, thrusting his opponent harmlessly to the ground with his lance.

But when he clashed with the second knight, he knew he had taken on a far more serious challenger. Little did he realize that Sir Percival, whom he had left behind at Camelot many years earlier as a young lad, had matured during his travels into one of the strongest and most fearsome fighters in the land.

Both knights were soon knocked off their horses, and the swordfight began.

Lancelot was an expert swordsman, and he fully expected to win. But his old, rusty black armor gave him a serious disadvantage against the strange newcomer, who was exceptionally light on his feet, and fought with a narrow, razor-sharp blade.

Both men received many wounds, but they fought on into the dusk, dodging and circling each other, darting forward and back, and thrilling the crowds with their artful swipes and skillful parries. At last, bleeding and breathless, they both sank exhausted onto the ground.

"A draw!" shouted the lord of the Isle, rushing over to where the Trespassing Knight and his valiant opponent lay panting on the trampled grass.

"I call a draw! No knight has lost his life today, Sir," he said, helping Lancelot up, "and it would be a terrible shame to end on a tragic note." Then he helped Percival up too.

"Well," the lord said, when they had both recovered, "I think I'll have to announce joint winners after all! Congratulations, Sir! Perhaps you won't be as shy as our Trespassing Knight, and will agree to tell us your name?"

"I am Sir Percival, of the Round Table," said Percival proudly, lifting off his helmet. "And this is my comrade, Sir Hector, the brother of Sir Lancelot."

There was a clatter as the Trespassing Knight dropped his sword.

"Everything all right, old chap?" asked the lord of the Joyous Isle. "Can't win 'em all, y'know!"

"Hector," Lancelot was saying, in a trembling whisper. "Percival. . ."

He suddenly tore off his big, black helmet and threw it on the ground. Then, with tears of joy in his eyes, he flung his arms around his long-lost friend and brother.

Some time later, Lancelot, Hector and Percival were back in the great hall at Camelot. Percival had convinced Lancelot that Arthur and Guinevere both missed him, and that everyone wanted him back, and at last they had managed to persuade him to go with them.

"So, only one question remains!" laughed Arthur jovially, as all the knights sat admiringly around Sir Lancelot. "What on earth made you run off like that?"

Lancelot stole a look at Guinevere, who cast her eyes down modestly. His heart filled with panic. He had absolutely no idea what to say.

"Well, I . . ." he mumbled uselessly.

"It was for the love of a lady, I believe, your majesty," interrupted Gawain, and Lancelot stared at him furiously, terrified that his secret love for Guinevere was about to be revealed.

But Gawain went on. "A lady called Elaine," he grinned. "He's told me all about it. Oh yes, Lancelot's always getting himself into romantic scrapes!"

Everyone, including Sir Lancelot, sighed with relief. Arthur seemed perfectly happy with the explanation. Stretching and yawning, the king stood up, and was about to say goodnight when there was a clattering noise at the gate.

In rode a big, burly knight, carrying a battered shield, and wearing armor that had certainly seen better days. He dismounted, bowed deeply to the king and queen, and took off his helmet.

"Do you remember me?" he asked, with a familiar smile.

Now that Sir Bors too had returned, the Round Table was once again complete. But it was not for very much longer that Arthur and his knights would sit together in Camelot as friends and comrades.

Everyone was delighted to have Lancelot back; but it was this that would eventually give Morgan le Fay the opportunity to achieve what she had desired for so long: the destruction of Camelot, and the end of King Arthur's reign.

CHAPTER FOURTEEN

SIR LOVELYHANDS

It was the feast of Pentecost, and King Arthur had declared, as he did every feast day, that he would not eat until he had seen or heard of some strange marvel, miracle or adventure. While the celebrations got under way inside, the king stood in the great gateway of Camelot, twiddling his thumbs and waiting for something to happen.

After a few minutes, he noticed someone strolling over the brow of the hill toward the castle. The figure came nearer, and Arthur could see that it was a very tall young man.

"Welcome!" the king cried cheerily. "What can I do for you?"

The boy bowed deeply, and Arthur couldn't help noticing that he was extremely handsome, and had the largest, most beautiful hands he had ever seen.

"Noble King Arthur!" said the youth politely. "May your kingdom be blessed, and may your knights prosper. I've come to ask you if you will give me three gifts."

Arthur was hungry. He looked the visitor up and down. Perhaps, he thought, just perhaps, the young man's arrival would lead to some interesting adventure.

He smiled graciously. "I will grant you your gifts," he said, in a grand tone of voice.

"Ask, and they shall be yours."

"Well," said the young man, "the first is, that you'll give me food and lodging for a year and a day. And then, at the end of that time, I'll ask for the two other things."

"Oh, come on!" said Arthur generously. "Ask for something better than that! I'm the king, after all, and you seem like a strong lad. I thought you were going to ask to be made a knight!"

"Food and lodging is all I want," said the boy. "If your majesty would be so kind."

"Oh, very well then," said Arthur, shaking his head, and the stranger followed him inside.

"Sir Kay," King Arthur announced above the noise of the banquet. "I want you to find a place for this young man, who wishes to stay with us for a year."

All the knights quietened down to stare at the new arrival. Everyone agreed that he looked tall and strong enough to make a fine knight, and many of them, especially the ladies, remarked on his lovely hands.

"They're so strong and manly," said Guinevere admiringly to her maid.

"What a shame he doesn't want to be a knight," said Sir Gawain. "With those hands, he'd make a great swordsman."

But Sir Kay merely took the young man into the kitchens, and told the cook that he'd found her a lad to help wash the dishes.

"See how that suits you, Lovelyhands," he said sarcastically. "If you had noble blood, you would have asked for a horse and armor, or to be made a knight. But if all you want is a job and a place to stay, you must be good for nothing."

The other knights thought it was a shame that such a fine young man had to work in the kitchens, instead of training to be a knight. But the boy seemed happy enough. Sir Kay's name for him, Lovelyhands, caught on, and soon that was what everyone was calling him. He hadn't told them his real name, after all.

The months went by, and Lovelyhands worked hard, washing pans and dishes, chopping vegetables and sweeping the floor.

The cook was delighted. She'd never had such a handsome, hard-working kitchen lad before. He got on with the other servants, and when they held games or competitions, he usually won. He loved to watch the knights practicing their jousting, and in his spare time he would practice too, using a stick for a sword and a tree for an enemy. Then Kay would laugh at him and say to the other knights, "How do you like my Sir Lovelyhands, the knight of the kitchen?"

But many of the knights felt sorry for Lovelyhands. Sir Lancelot and Sir Gawain secretly offered him pieces of gold and fine clothes, but Lovelyhands always politely refused. "I have everything I've asked for," he would say.

"Perhaps he *is* just a kitchen boy, and nothing more," Gawain sighed. But he couldn't help thinking there was something noble and knightly in the young man.

Winter came, and winter turned to spring, and eventually the feast of Pentecost came around once more. Lovelyhands was busy at the stove stirring delicious soups and sauces for the grand banquet, the knights were gathering in the hall, and King Arthur, as usual, was standing at the gate, on the lookout for an exciting event.

"Well, I hope we're in for something a little more interesting than what happened last year," he mumbled.

"King Arthur!" cried a woman's voice. Arthur had been so busy talking to himself that he hadn't noticed the damsel who had approached him.

"I come to beg the assistance of the Knights of the Round Table," she said, an anguished look on her face. "It's an emergency!"

"Come in, come in," said Arthur, ushering her into the hall. He called for silence and asked the lady what she needed.

"My sister is being besieged!" said the damsel. "The Red Knight of the Red Lands is surrounding her castle with an army of knights. He says he won't stop unless he can have a battle with a Knight of the Round Table. And if he wins, he says he'll carry my sister away to the Red Lands!" wailed the lady, starting to cry. "I need a really excellent knight to help me," she sobbed.

"What is your sister's name, and where does she live?" asked Arthur gently.

"Well. . . I can't tell you that just now," said the damsel. "But I can assure you that she *is* a noble lady."

Arthur's eyes narrowed slightly. He suspected a trap, set by his evil half-sister, Morgan le Fay.

"If you can't tell me her name," he said, "then I'm sorry, but I can't let any of my knights go with you."

"But I *need* a Knight of the Round Table!" complained the damsel indignantly.

"I'll go," said a deep, gentle voice from the other side of the hall.

It was Lovelyhands. He had come out of the kitchen and was listening to the goings-on in the hall. His sleeves were rolled up and he was carrying a dirty ladle.

"What?" said Arthur.

"It's been a year and a day, your majesty," said Lovelyhands calmly, "and I'd like to ask for my next two gifts. One is that you make me a Knight of the Round Table. I would like to be knighted by Sir Lancelot. And the other is that you allow me to take on this adventure, to rescue this lady's sister from the Red Knight of the Red Lands."

Arthur had promised that he would grant the young man his three wishes, and he could not go back on his word. So he asked Sir Lancelot to find Lovelyhands some armor and a horse, and to make him a knight as soon as possible.

"Is that all I get?" moaned the damsel. "A kitchen boy? A dish washer?"

"If you're going to be a true knight," said Lancelot, helping Lovelyhands with his armor, "you must tell me your real name."

"I will tell you, but it's a secret," said Lovelyhands. "My real name is Gareth, and I am Sir Gawain's brother ~ although he doesn't know I exist. I was born a long time after him, when he had left home. You mustn't tell anyone. I don't want anyone to know until I've proved my worth by myself."

Lancelot smiled, and touched the boy's shoulder with his sword.

"Arise, Sir Gareth," he said solemnly. "Or should I say, 'Sir Lovelyhands'. May you bring glory to the Round Table. Your secret's safe with me."

"Huh!" grumbled the damsel, sitting behind Sir Lovelyhands on his horse as they trotted away from Camelot. "Just my luck to get a kitchen boy to be my knight," she said meanly, prodding him in the back. "Fat lot of use *you'll* be!"

"Say what you like," answered Lovelyhands calmly, "but I've accepted this adventure on behalf of the Round Table, and I will see it through to the end."

They rode on through the forest until they came across a terrified-looking man tearing through the undergrowth, as if his life depended on it.

"Oh, Sir, please help me!" he panted. "My lord has been kidnapped by six thieves, and I'm afraid they'll kill him!"

Lovelyhands rode after the man, and found the lord tied up with the thieves standing all around him.

"Get away from him!" he shouted, drawing his sword. "Leave him alone!" And he fought the thieves until three of them lay dead and the other three had run for their lives into the forest. Then he cut the ropes to free the grateful lord, who begged him to come back to his castle where he could give him a reward.

"I ask no reward," said Lovelyhands. "I am a Knight of the Round Table, and I am on a quest to help this lady."

"I suppose you think I'm impressed?" said the damsel scornfully as they rode on through the forest. "Well, that was just good luck you had back there. You're still a kitchen boy, and you stink of smoke and grease. Wait till you meet the Red Knight of the Red Lands ~ you'll have no chance!"

On and on they rode, across wide rivers, past overhanging cliffs and through flower-filled meadows, with the maiden constantly complaining and insulting Lovelyhands. But when they came to a strange black tree, with a black flag and a black shield hanging in its branches, she suddenly looked very frightened.

"Quick!" she whispered, "run away down the valley! Don't let him see us!"

"Don't let *who* see us?" asked Sir Lovelyhands with a puzzled frown. He couldn't see anyone.

"The Black Knight!" said the lady, her eyes almost popping with fright. "He really *will* kill you. I'm not joking!"

"I'm no coward," said Lovelyhands. "Black Knight! Where are you? Come out and fight!"

"Who are YOU?" roared a gruff voice, and out from behind the tree stepped a huge knight with a thick, black beard.

"He's just a kitchen boy," said the damsel quickly. "Take no notice!"

"What's he doing with *you* then?" growled the Black Knight. "No kitchen boy would ride with such a lady!"

"I'm a noble knight!" Lovelyhands insisted.

"Hah! Prove it then!" laughed the Black Knight nastily, taking his shield down from the tree. Lovelyhands quickly helped the lady down from his horse and prepared to joust with the Black Knight.

No sooner had he lifted up his lance than the knight charged toward him at breakneck speed, his head down. Lovelyhands urged his horse forward, and the two fighters smashed together with an almighty CRUNCH! Lovelyhands's lance tore through his enemy's armor and wounded him badly in the side, and both men were knocked off their horses, but the Black Knight still drew his sword and lunged forward.

They fought viciously, their swords clanging and scraping, until at last the Black Knight began to lose strength. His wound bleeding heavily, he finally sank weakly onto the dry leaves on the forest floor.

"Do you yield now, Sir Knight?" Lovelyhands demanded. But when he looked a little more closely, he saw that the Black Knight was dead.

"Now do you believe I'm a brave and noble knight?" asked Lovelyhands, as he and the damsel rode on side by side. Lovelyhands had taken the Black Knight's black horse and armor, and given his own horse to the lady.

"I can't believe a stupid kitchen boy killed the Black Knight," sulked the damsel. "It must have been a fluke. You think you're so clever, but just you wait until you meet the Red Knight of the Red Lands! You'll be no match for him! Kitchen boy!" she snorted.

Lovelyhands rolled his eyes and said nothing.

After a while, they saw another knight coming in the opposite direction. He and his horse were dressed all in bright green.

"Now you've had it!" whispered the damsel. "That's the Green Knight, and he's not going to be in a very good mood when he hears what you've done."

"Well, if it isn't my brother, the Black Knight!" called the Green Knight. "How are you? I haven't seen you for ages!"

"I'm not the Black Knight," said Lovelyhands bravely. "I am Sir Lovelyhands of the Round Table, and I have slain your brother in honest combat and taken his armor."

"He's just a kitchen boy," put in the damsel hurriedly. But the Green Knight was staring at them in horror and fury.

"You've done *what*?" he fumed. "You've *killed my brother*? I'll pay you back for that! I'll KILL you. I'll RIP you to PIECES!" He immediately charged at Lovelyhands, knocking him completely off his horse with his lance before Lovelyhands could even get

They fought viciously, their swords clanging and scraping. . .

ready to fight. Swiftly drawing his sword, Lovelyhands ran behind the Green Knight and grabbed his leg, pulling him off his horse. Then the two knights began to duel, swiping and stabbing at each other with their swords.

Lovelyhands was not doing very well. First the Green Knight caught him with a painful stroke on the arm, and then delivered a massive blow that broke his shield in two. This made Lovelyhands so furious that he leaped forward and brought his sword down right on top of the Green Knight's helmet.

The Green Knight swayed dizzily and dropped onto his knees. Lovelyhands quickly kicked him onto his back, stood on his chest and pointed his sword at his throat.

"Mercy!" wailed the knight. "Spare me, and I will give you thirty knights, and follow you as your loyal servant!"

"I will spare you," said Lovelyhands, "if this lady asks me to."

"Huh!" said the damsel. "To think that a kitchen boy should have thirty knights to follow him! It's ridiculous."

"Please," groaned the Green Knight miserably.

"Oh, all right then," said the lady. "Spare him."

"Your wish is my command," said Sir Lovelyhands, helping the Green Knight up.

Soon Lovelyhands and the damsel were once again riding on their way. Behind them rode the Green Knight, and behind him rode the thirty knights he had given to Sir Lovelyhands.

They certainly made an amazing sight trotting through the forest, their harnesses jangling and their armor glinting in the sun. All the peasants and woodcutters who saw them pass by waved and doffed their caps, thinking that Sir Lovelyhands and his knights must be a grand royal party out for a ride.

But still the damsel kept moaning and complaining, saying that Lovelyhands was nothing but a kitchen boy who was unworthy to serve her.

"I don't know why I bothered going to Camelot at all," she huffed, "when all they could offer was a useless—"

She was interrupted by a loud trumpet blast that made the leaves tremble.

Up ahead was a huge clearing, filled with beautiful striped pavilions and crowds of jostling spectators. In the middle was a neatly mown jousting field.

"Ah!" said the Green Knight, "I know what this is. My other brother, the Indigo Knight, has organized a tournament. And a noble Knight of the Round Table, such as yourself," he added, turning to Sir Lovelyhands, "wouldn't turn down the opportunity to fight at such a grand event, now would you?"

The damsel, wearing a bored expression, watched from the best seats as Sir Lovelyhands took part in the tournament. She saw him defeat many bold and brave opponents with his cunning, strength and agility, until at last it was time for Lovelyhands to fight the Indigo Knight himself.

The Green Knight had told his brother all about how Lovelyhands had defeated him and killed their brother,

the Black Knight. And although the Indigo Knight was noble and honest, he was angry, and determined to get his revenge.

The crowd was tense with excitement as Sir Lovelyhands faced his opponent. The Indigo Knight and his horse were both dressed in armor of the deepest, darkest blue, and a long, indigo plume waved from the top of his helmet.

The two knights charged at each other, their horses' hooves pounding the turf as they thundered closer and closer together.

They met with a loud crash, shoving each other violently onto the ground. The crowd started to cheer and shout, yelling the names of their favorites to win the battle. The Indigo Knight drew a long silvery sword inlaid with deep blue stones, while Lovelyhands drew the sturdy sword that Sir Lancelot had given him.

Never had the crowd seen such an exciting duel. Both knights were excellent swordsmen, and their blades clashed and clanged so swiftly that they appeared as a blur of shining metal. To and fro they battled over the grass, jabbing and slashing at each other, until, finally, Sir Lovelyhands managed to strike the Indigo Knight so hard on the arm that he dropped his sword.

"Yes!" screamed the damsel despite herself, leaping up in excitement as Lovelyhands chased his enemy around the field, eventually catching up with him and wrestling him to the ground.

"I've never met such a knight as you," confessed the Indigo Knight, after they had shaken hands and taken off their helmets. "And, if I may, I'd like to ask to join you as your follower. I can offer you ninety brave knights as a token of my loyalty."

A few days later, Sir Lovelyhands, the damsel and all their retinue drew near to the castle where the Red Knight of the Red Lands was besieging the damsel's sister.

They sent a knight ahead of them to announce their arrival, and soon he came riding back through the forest with a message from the Red Knight.

"He says he doesn't want to fight just *any* Knight of the Round Table," panted the knight. "He say's it's got to be Sir Lancelot, Sir Tristram or Sir Gawain."

"Well," said Sir Lovelyhands, "you can tell him that I am Sir Gareth, Sir Gawain's brother, and that I've defeated the Black Knight, the Green Knight and the Indigo Knight." Looking surprised, the messenger headed back, and Lovelyhands turned to the damsel beside him.

"*Now* do you believe I'm a noble knight?" he asked.

The damsel pretended not to have heard him. "Oh look!" she said breezily, pointing through the trees. "We're here! There's my sister at the window!"

They came out into a lush open meadow, where the Red Knight's soldiers were camped all around a gleaming white castle. As they approached, Lovelyhands suddenly spotted a stunningly beautiful lady, with curly brown hair and large, worried-looking eyes, leaning out of a window high up in the castle wall.

"Lyonet!" called the damsel. "It's all right! We're here!"

"Lyones!" the lady in the castle called back, in a soft, sweet voice that sent a tingle down Lovelyhands's spine. "Have you got a Knight of the Round Table to fight for me?"

The damsel nodded and pointed at Lovelyhands. But he was staring, unable to speak. He had fought many battles, and proved how strong, brave and clever he was. But never before had he fallen in love.

"Are you ready?" asked the damsel.

"I . . . I . . ." stuttered Lovelyhands. He stared at the lovely face at the window, feeling strangely dizzy. He was suffused with an amazing desire to save Lady Lyonet. He would fight whoever stood in his way, if only he could have her safely in his arms.

"So!" growled a sarcastic voice in his ear. "You're the bold, heroic Knight of the Round Table who's come to take me on, are you?"

Standing next to him, Lovelyhands saw a knight with a chest as broad as a barrel, shiny red armor, and thick, tufty red hair sprouting from his head, chin and nostrils.

"Or should I say, the doomed and *foolish* knight!" chortled the Red Knight of the Red Lands. "You'll never defeat me!"

Lovelyhands faced the Red Knight on the meadow beneath Lady Lyonet's window. At one end of the field stood the Red Knight's armies, cheering him on. Behind Lovelyhands stood the damsel, the Green Knight, the Indigo Knight and all their followers.

"Come on then, if you think you're brave enough!" roared the Red Knight viciously. Lovelyhands gathered his thoughts, gripped his lance, and took one last look up at the window where Lady Lyonet stood. Love surged through him as he gazed at her anxious face, and he secretly blew her a tiny kiss.

Then, quick as the blink of an eye, he saw his lady mouth three words to him:

"I love you."

That was all Lovelyhands needed. Determined to save his lady, he thundered toward the Red Knight harder and faster than he had ever charged before. He planted his lance squarely in the middle of the Red Knight's stomach, sending him sailing several yards across the meadow, to land in a crumpled heap next to the castle wall.

Then Lovelyhands hopped off his horse, quickly drew his sword, and was standing over his enemy with the blade pointed at his chest before the Red Knight of the Red Lands even knew where he was.

All his knights leaped into the air shouting and yelling with excitement, while the Red Knight's armies disappointedly began to pack up their tents and battering rams.

The Red Knight picked himself up and reluctantly shook Lovelyhands by the hand.

"Well done," he mumbled. "The castle is yours, I suppose." And with that he shuffled off to join his troops, and they were soon heading off into the forest.

But Lovelyhands was only interested in his lady. He kicked down the castle door, bounded up the white stone steps and ran to find Lyonet, who was waiting for him with her arms outstretched. They embraced each other like long-lost lovers, and then Lovelyhands immediately kneeled down and begged Lady Lyonet to marry him.

And that was how Lovelyhands, the humble knight of the kitchen, came to be heading over the brow of the hill to Camelot once again, this time with his new wife, her sister, and a troop of one hundred and twenty-two noble knights.

King Arthur, strolling absent-mindedly near the gate, could hardly believe his eyes when he saw the ranks of warriors in their glittering armor, the beautiful lady, and the tall, oddly familiar knight who led the way.

"Welcome!" the king shouted, as he always did. "And how can I help you, noble— Lovelyhands! It *is* Lovelyhands, isn't it?"

"It *was*," said the knight, smiling warmly. "But now I can tell you my real name. I am Sir Gareth ~ brother to Sir Gawain, and fit to be called a Knight of the Round Table."

CHAPTER FIFTEEN

LANCELOT AND GUINEVERE

It had been over a year since Lancelot had returned to Camelot, and everyone was glad he had come home. The king had his best knight back, and the other knights were overjoyed to be reunited with their friend. But the person who was happiest of all was Guinevere.

When her handsome knight had returned home after so long, the queen had at first been careful to greet him with cold, formal politeness. Sir Lancelot, for his part, had merely kissed her hand and said he would be proud to be allowed to serve her once more.

But, in private, their love for each other had never waned. Every time Lancelot was away from Camelot, the queen grew restless. Each time he returned unharmed from his latest exploit, she found it harder and harder to conceal her delight and relief. And in the end, their friendship did not go entirely unnoticed at Camelot.

Stableboys and grooms began to remark upon how often the pair went riding together. Two Knights of the Round Table, Sir Agravain and Sir Mordred, could often be seen whispering in dark corners. Cooks and maids chattered on the stairs. But any rumors that reached the king's ears were swiftly dismissed as groundless gossip, and Merlin's old warnings about Guinevere went unheeded. Until one fateful day. . .

Sir Mordred had come to court as a young squire, while Sir Lancelot had been missing. The young man's name seemed vaguely familiar to Arthur from something Merlin had once said, but the king cast any doubts aside and accepted him willingly into the fellowship of the Round Table. What Arthur did not know was that Mordred had been sent there by Morgan le Fay, to make trouble. Beneath the façade of loyal knight and trusted friend was hidden a deep and savage hatred of Arthur, and a fanatical jealousy of Lancelot.

"My day will come," said Mordred to Morgan le Fay at one of their secret meetings.

"Indeed it will," said the sorceress. "Your day will come soon."

Sir Lancelot was still the best knight at Camelot, and he remained Arthur's favorite. But Lancelot knew he could never be truly noble as long as he loved the queen. He became convinced that the only way to extinguish his passion was to try to avoid her as much as possible. So he jumped at any chance to leave Camelot on a mission or quest, sometimes spending long, lonely days just riding through the forest. The queen soon noticed his frequent absences and reluctance to spend time with her.

"You've grown cold toward me," she said to him one spring day. "Have you fallen for another lady now?"

"You know I could never love another," replied Lancelot. "But you're still the wife of my best friend and king. How can I ever be a good knight when I love another man's wife? I'm just trying to avoid the pain that our meetings bring to both of us. . . and to preserve your good name. You know people are talking."

"But it's all lies!" shouted Guinevere. "You know we have nothing to be ashamed of. You're just tired of me! Well I'm tired too ~ tired of never knowing where you are and tired of waiting for you to return. How can you protect me when you're hardly ever here?"

Lancelot protested that he was still her protector, but his arguments fell on deaf ears. The queen was too upset to listen and told him to leave at once. Lancelot went straight to the stables, saddled his horse and rode sadly into the forest.

Guinevere soon bitterly regretted her angry words and wanted to apologize to Lancelot, but she couldn't. Nobody knew where he was.

The next day, when Lancelot had still not returned, the queen decided to go riding in the woods. She did not reveal to the maids and knights who accompanied her the real reason for the outing ~ to look for her beloved knight.

"This is my favorite time of year," said Guinevere, as they trotted through a sea of bluebells in the dappled sunlight.

"Is that because it's a time for lovers?" said one of her ladies with a little giggle.

Suddenly an arrow whizzed past her ear, and Guinevere froze. Her eyes darted rapidly from one side to the other, and she realized with horror that they were surrounded by soldiers. Armed men on horseback stood poised among the trees on all sides, while scores of archers, their bows at the ready, lurked behind the bushes that grew on the forest floor.

"Do not attempt to fight us," said a voice behind her. Guinevere spun around.

It was Sir Melligrance, a Knight of the Round Table. He had long been enamored of Guinevere, but she felt nothing for him except loathing. What he couldn't get by natural appeal he had decided to take by force, and with Lancelot away and Guinevere deep in the forest, he had at last seen his chance to kidnap her.

The queen's knights did their best to defend her from Melligrance's clutches, but they were not even wearing their armor, so the battle easily went against them. Within minutes, they all lay sprawling and injured on the ground. Melligrance's men waded in through the flowers to finish them off.

"Stop!" screamed Guinevere. "Don't kill them. I'll do whatever you want, but please spare my knights and servants."

"Then come to my castle without a struggle," said Melligrance, with a wicked smirk.

As the party was led off through the forest, a brave young maid slipped away unnoticed from the back of the group and sprinted off through the trees.

Queen Guinevere looked out of the window from the high tower where she was held captive.

"Look!" she said to her maid. A farmer's cart was approaching the castle at an alarming speed, swaying from side to side and nearly overturning each time it took a bend. As it drew closer, Guinevere let out a cry of excitement.

"It's him!"

"Who, Madam?"

"Sir Lancelot, of course!" cried Guinevere delightedly.

Lancelot's sudden arrival took the castle guards by surprise, and he was inside the walls before they could start raising the drawbridge. Like an angry bull, he charged across the courtyard, impervious to the arrows of the bowmen on the ramparts. Fighting off every swordsman who crossed his path, he quickly gained access to the castle and rampaged through the narrow passageways, bellowing at the top of his voice:

"Cowardly cur! Hound from hell! Treacherous viper! Where are you, Melligrance? Come out and fight." When Melligrance recognized Lancelot's voice, he ran straight to the queen.

"Help me!" he begged. "He'll kill me."

"Why should I help you, you traitor?" said Guinevere haughtily.

"I spared your knights ~ please remember that. I'll do whatever you want."

"All I want is my freedom," said Guinevere. Lancelot could now be heard at the foot of the spiral stairway leading up to the tower:

"Loathsome slug! Barbarous brute! Slimy reptile!" His insults thundered up the staircase. He was just about to storm up the steps.

Melligrance opened the door, shoved Guinevere unceremoniously out, and slammed it shut behind her. She came tumbling down the stone stairway and landed safely in Lancelot's arms. As soon as he'd made sure she was unhurt, Lancelot bounded up the last flight of steps and flung open the door. The room was empty, except for the maid cowering in the corner.

"Where is the vile toad?" he yelled.

The maid raised her eyes to the rafters and screamed as, with a loud cry, Melligrance leaped onto Lancelot's back and began to tighten his arms around his neck. Quick as a flash, Lancelot reached up and grabbed the traitor's arms. Then he bent forward, flipped him over his head like a rag doll and dashed him to the floor. The defeated kidnapper lay on his back, winded and whimpering with pain. In an instant, the point of Lancelot's sword was at his throat.

"No!" croaked Melligrance.

"No!" echoed a voice in the doorway. It was Guinevere. "He spared my knights. He doesn't deserve to die."

Lancelot did not move. His eyes were wild with fury. Sweat was pouring down his face and his chest was heaving. The injured knight lay rigid and motionless on the floor, white with terror. His bulging eyes stared up at Lancelot.

"Be merciful, Lancelot," said the queen softly. Lancelot lifted his sword barely an inch.

"If you ever come anywhere near the queen again, I'll make mincemeat of you," he snarled. "Do you understand?"

"Yes," whispered Melligrance.

"How did you know where to find me?" Guinevere asked Lancelot when they were on their way back to Camelot.

"It was your maid," replied Lancelot. "I was riding up the hill to Camelot, when she hurtled through a hedge onto the road in front of me. I nearly knocked her down! As soon as she'd explained what had happened, I shot off to rescue you, but my horse was felled by an archer before I got anywhere near the castle, so I grabbed the farm cart for the final stretch."

"I knew you would come," said Guinevere with an affectionate smile. "My knight in the cart!"

The story of Lancelot's daring rescue reached Camelot before he did, and he returned with Guinevere to a hero's welcome. In front of the whole court, Arthur thanked him for saving the queen from Melligrance's evil intentions.

With all the excitement, Guinevere had still not had the chance to apologize to Lancelot for her angry words, so she arranged to meet him secretly in the garden that evening.

But they were not the only ones taking the air that night. Sir Mordred, spurred on by his jealousy of Lancelot, who it seemed could do no wrong in the king's eyes, had decided it was time to take action.

With his accomplice, Sir Agravain, he had followed Lancelot into the garden and hidden behind a thick hedge to spy on the couple and listen to their words of love.

"Come to my chamber tonight," they heard the queen whisper. It was exactly what they wanted to hear.

"They're traitors!" cried Mordred triumphantly, bursting into Arthur's chamber later the same night, without even bothering to knock.

"What are you talking about, Mordred?" asked Arthur calmly.

"Sir Lancelot and the queen. We caught them together in her chamber this evening. We have witnesses to prove it!" crowed Mordred.

Arthur stared at Mordred long and hard before responding.

"Tell me more," he said finally. His face had hardened, but there were tears in his eyes.

"Lancelot escaped, but we've arrested the queen," said Mordred. "She's sitting in the dungeon as we speak. And you know the punishment for infidelity as well as I do. The queen must die!"

Arthur's head was lowered, and his eyes were downcast. A few tears splashed onto the grey stone floor.

For his whole marriage, he had tried to ignore suggestions that his wife was not entirely faithful. He had pretended not to see the look in her eye when Lancelot came into view, and had told himself not to worry when both of them disappeared for hours on end. He loved Guinevere, and he was reluctant to challenge her. Nor could he bear to confront Sir Lancelot, who was his best friend and his bravest knight.

But now he could no longer deny that he had been made a fool of, and he would have to do something. If he didn't act soon, and firmly, no one would respect his leadership.

"I cannot make exceptions. . . even for my own wife," he sobbed quietly. Gulping back the tears, he drew himself up to his full height and looked Mordred in the face. "The laws of the land must be upheld. Do what has to be done."

And so it was that one gray, misty morning a few days later, Guinevere, blindfolded and dressed in a tattered linen robe, was led out into the marketplace to be burned at the stake.

A priest administered the last rites, and then the queen was hauled up onto the pyre of sticks and brushwood and tied firmly to the stake with thick ropes. But she refused to show any shame or regret, for she knew she had done nothing wrong. Even when she smelled the acrid smoke from the torch, as it was carried solemnly across the flagstones, she held her head high.

Mordred and his armed men encircled the unlit bonfire. The other knights, unarmed and clothed in black, stood behind them with their heads bowed.

Of the whole court, King Arthur alone was absent. He was spending the fateful day in his chambers, as he couldn't bear to witness the execution of his once beloved wife. Only the heartbroken weeping of Guinevere's loyal maids broke the sorrowful silence.

As the bearer of the torch neared the center of the square, there was a stirring at the back of the crowd. The sea of bodies suddenly parted to let through a band of knights, galloping toward the queen at breakneck speed.

Mordred and his crew scarcely had time to draw their swords before the knights had forced their way through to the fire, cutting down anyone who stood in their path. The leader of the group, riding a mighty stallion, leaped from his mount onto the pyre, and, using his razor sharp sword, swiftly slashed the bonds that tied Guinevere to the stake. Then, as his men fought off any remaining opponents, he carefully eased off her blindfold.

"Lancelot!" sobbed Guinevere, recognizing her rescuer as he lifted her gently onto his horse. The knight in shining armor swept back across the marketplace, like a furious whirlwind, leaving injured and dying knights in his wake. His band of followers met no resistance as they charged after him, heading for his castle.

Over forty knights were killed on that terrible day. Among them were Sir Tor, Sir Gryflet, and Sir Gawain's two beloved brothers, Sir Gaheris and Sir Gareth.

The loss of so many lives wreaked havoc on the Round Table, as the knights split into opposing camps. Many supported Arthur and blamed Lancelot for betraying his king and slaughtering so many of his former friends. Those who had lost close comrades were eager to avenge them, and they burned with hatred for Sir Lancelot.

Others, however, were worried about Sir Mordred and his sinister influence on King Arthur. They could not really believe that the knight had caught the lovers together, and they thought Arthur had been foolish to listen to him.

In the end, a large proportion of the Knights of the Round Table abandoned the king, and switched their allegiance to Sir Lancelot. They set off for his castle, miles away from Camelot, to join him. They sensed that the years of fame and glory for King Arthur and the Knights of the Round Table were finally nearing their end, and that the Kingdom of Logres was plunging once more into chaos.

That left a third group ~ Mordred and his followers, who were receiving their instructions from Morgan le Fay. Surveying the wreckage of Arthur's court, once the most powerful gathering of knights in the world, the wicked sorceress saw her chance. She would stop at nothing to bring about the downfall of the Round Table. Sir Lancelot and the king were now enemies. The time for retribution had come.

The knight in shining armor swept back across the marketplace. . . .

CHAPTER SIXTEEN

THE LAST BATTLE

Sir Gawain stared at the young messenger in disbelief. His whole body began to tremble as the terrible truth hit home.

"Both of them?" he said, ashen faced. The messenger nodded his head solemnly, not daring to look Gawain in the face.

"Dead?" said Gawain.

The messenger's answer was drowned out by an almighty wail of deep despair that tore through the castle walls and out into the valleys below. Shepherds were shaken from their hillside slumbers. Wolves were roused from their lairs and a horrible howling swept down the mountainside and into the villages, to be answered by the baying of every dog for miles around. It was as if the kingdom had been ripped savagely apart by the grievous news.

"Sir Gareth and Sir Gaheris were killed by Sir Lancelot this morning," repeated the messenger slowly. His duty done, he turned to the door. No words could bring back the great knight's beloved brothers or alleviate his sorrow. The simple message had already inflicted a wound too deep to heal.

If Gawain's desperate, driving desire for revenge had not fixed itself so firmly in his heart, like the sword into the stone; if Arthur had not been so deeply moved by his

nephew's grief and by his own sorrow at the loss of his knights and the betrayal of his wife, perhaps it would have been possible to prevent the terrible chain of events which followed. But when the king rushed in to see what poor, pain-racked creature had uttered that awful cry, and saw his nephew's tortured face screaming for revenge, he knew what he had to do.

He quickly called together the remaining Knights of the Round Table and summoned a great army to lay siege to Sir Lancelot's castle. For fourteen long summer weeks, they camped out around the walls. Every day Arthur would call for silence and challenge Lancelot to fight, and for fourteen long weeks his appeals were met only by the cries of swallows and the calls of corncrakes. On the hundredth day of the siege, when the reapers were bringing the harvest home, a tall figure with long, flowing hair appeared on the battlements. At first Arthur did not recognize his former friend ~ he looked so gaunt and weary. But Lancelot it was.

"Send your men home, Arthur," he called. "I will not fight my own king."

"We are enemies now, Sir Lancelot," replied Arthur gravely. "And though I would not wish it so, I cannot forgive you for killing my knights, for abducting my wife, or for your betrayal. It's time for justice to be done. Come out and fight."

"I killed your knights to save *your* queen," shouted Lancelot, "from the horrible death *you* had sentenced her to. If you could only see reason, you wouldn't listen to the lies of traitors, but would welcome her back with open arms."

"Murderer! Liar! Coward!" shrieked a voice from below. It belonged to Sir Gawain. He was red in the face and spitting with rage. "You killed my brothers . . . my unarmed brothers. You deserve to die, you dog. I want revenge and I will not rest until I have it. Come out and fight!"

Lancelot tried to reason with Gawain. He told him that he had not recognized Gareth and Gaheris. He

said that he did not want to fight, but the grief-stricken knight was implacable. So Lancelot tried one last, desperate appeal to the king:

"Please stop this madness. No good can possibly come of it. We don't have to be set against each other like fighting dogs. I beg of you, Arthur, withdraw."

It is said that the king would have made peace with Lancelot there and then, if it had not been for Gawain's insistence on revenge. But the younger man could not be appeased. With a never-ending stream of invective, he incited everyone around to challenge Lancelot again and again, until a terrible battle ensued.

Old friends who had shared so many adventures, so many meals and so many years of glory were set against each other in deadly combat. Many were killed. Gawain and his men concentrated their attack upon Lancelot, but Lancelot's knights managed to repel them every time. Even in the heat of battle, the greatest fighter in the land refused to strike out at his one-time ally.

Finally Arthur was knocked off his horse by Sir Bors, who was just about to strike a fatal blow when Lancelot grabbed his arm. "I cannot bear to see my king killed by a friend," he hissed. Then, above the uproar, and still holding Bors firmly by the arm, he shouted to Arthur:

"For God's sake, Arthur, this cannot go on. Please see reason!"

"Take Guinevere. Take my men. Take my life if you must, but put an end to this hatred. It's breaking my heart."

"I will stop the fighting," said Arthur, remounting his horse, "if Guinevere returns to me, and if you leave my kingdom forever. I cannot find it in my heart to forgive you."

Lancelot agreed to these conditions, and both men ordered their armies to withdraw. Gawain had been wounded and was too weak and exhausted to protest. Guinevere was led out of the castle. As she crossed the drawbridge, she couldn't resist a final glance back at her beloved knight as he started his preparations for exile in Gaul.

The peace which reigned over Logres after Lancelot's departure from the kingdom was short-lived and troubled. Sir Gawain was inconsolable and brooded relentlessly on his brothers' deaths. Mordred, as usual, leaped on any opportunity to stir up hatred against Lancelot; and finally, so many of the knights were siding with

Gawain and Mordred and demanding revenge, that Arthur had no choice but to declare war on Lancelot again. He summoned his men and set sail for Benwick Castle ~ Lancelot's new home across the sea in Gaul ~ leaving Mordred to rule in his absence.

It was the moment Mordred had been waiting for. No sooner had Arthur set sail than he gathered his own army and announced that he had been chosen as heir to the throne, as Arthur had been killed at Benwick. He summoned the Archbishop, and bullied him into performing a hasty coronation. Then he tried to force Guinevere to marry him. Somehow she managed to escape and sought refuge in a high tower, protected by a few faithful followers. From there, she succeeded in getting this message to Arthur:

COME QUICKLY.
MORDRED HAS USURPED
THRONE. KINGDOM
IN DANGER.

As soon as Arthur read this, he started back for Logres. All that the siege of Benwick had achieved was the death of even more men. Gawain and Lancelot had fought each other three times and each time Gawain had been wounded. By the time he reached the shores of Logres and tried to mount Gringalet, his old war horse, he was so weak that he collapsed on the beach. A low groan alerted Arthur. He raced over to see who was in trouble and saw Gawain lying face down in a pool of bloody water. Arthur turned him over.

"Forgive me," spluttered Gawain, recognizing his uncle. "It's all my fault ~ the killing and hatred. All so pointless. If it wasn't for me, Lancelot would be here now. I don't want to die his enemy."

"Then tell him," said Arthur, pulling a quill pen from his saddlebag. "I'll write to him. Tell me what to say." So Gawain, through his pain and tears, wrote this letter:

I am about to die from a wound you gave me at Benwick. Please don't let me die your enemy. I know now that my death is my own fault. My futile desire for revenge forced you into battle. I ask for your forgiveness and that you hurry to Arthur's aid with the largest army you can muster. Logres is in danger. Mordred has seized the throne. Arthur needs you. Come quickly, noble Lancelot.

Gawain

With these words, Gawain took his last breath. Arthur sat by his side through the long, dark night and cried until dawn finally broke above the majestic chalk cliffs that towered over the beach.

Five nights later, Arthur's army was encamped not far from Lake Avalon, where Arthur had first found Excalibur. Mordred and his men were camped across the plain, less than a mile away. While Arthur was in Gaul, they had marched into the south-west of Logres, seizing land and property and terrorizing anyone who would not join their army.

It was a cold, blustery night and Arthur could not sleep. In the morning he was to lead his men into battle ~ a battle which he feared would be his last. If Lancelot, Gawain and all the other Knights of the Round Table had still been with him, he would not have been so fearful of the outcome. But he had lost so many good fighters, and the men he had left were untrained and badly outnumbered.

As he mulled all this over, he became aware of a strange orange glow in the entrance of the tent. He looked up to see a tall, dark figure hovering in the doorway.

"Who's there?" he called.

"It's me, Uncle," said a faint, familiar voice.

"Gawain?" gasped Arthur in amazement. "But I thought you were. . ."

"I am, Uncle, but I have come back to warn you."

"Warn me? Of what?"

"If you do battle with Sir Mordred tomorrow, you will both be killed, together with all your men. You must make a truce on whatever terms you can. Within a week, Lancelot will be here and then you'll conquer Mordred. If you fight before then, it will end in disaster. Take heed, Uncle, or you won't have a chance."

"How do you know this?" asked Arthur. The ghostly figure was fading fast.

"Take heed," said the echoing voice again.

"Gawain. . ." called Arthur, but the ghost had vanished.

As soon as it was light, Arthur sent a message to Mordred, asking to meet him halfway between the two camps. Mordred complied, and one hour later the two men approached each other, unaccompanied and unarmed. Mordred agreed to a week's truce, if he could retain the south-west of Logres and have the whole kingdom after Arthur's death. Remembering Gawain's words, Arthur accepted, and both agreed that if any sword were drawn before the week was up, they would take it as a sign that the treaty had been broken.

For two days an uneasy peace reigned over the plain. Arthur paced up and down through the camp, anxiously scanning the horizon for any sign of Lancelot's arrival. His men kept their eyes fixed firmly on the enemy's distant tents, ready to respond to any sign of provocation. On the third day, Mordred's men were growing restless. It had become hot and humid and the prospect of putting on their heavy armor and spending another day in the sun waiting for something to happen was not at all appealing.

One of the knights was putting on his tunic, when he felt a sharp sting on his left foot. Looking down, he saw that he had trodden on a snake. Without thinking, he drew his sword to finish the animal off. Away across the plain, Arthur's men saw the blade flashing in the sunlight. A great cry went up and within seconds both armies were charging across the plain and into battle.

Centuries later, that last battle was still remembered as the fiercest that Logres had ever seen. All the long day it raged under the hot sun, as men struck out at their enemies in a fevered frenzy of killing. The thirst for blood and the desire for death seemed insatiable, as blow after blow came raining down. Blood-covered swords and dented shields clashed again and again. Toppled knights and horses came crashing down to their deaths on the dusty, sun-baked ground.

At dusk, the clatter of weapons, the neighing of wounded horses and the groans of dying men gave way to an eerie silence ~ the silence of death. King Arthur rode among the corpses of his

friends and enemies, weeping in despair at the tragic, pointless devastation. Of his men, only Sir Bedivere and Sir Lucan were left alive, and both were badly wounded.

Suddenly, he caught sight of Mordred, sitting on top of a heap of bodies, carefully wiping the blood off his sword.

"Give me my spear," he said to Lucan under his breath. Gripping the spear like a javelin, Arthur charged at Mordred with a blood-curdling cry.

When Mordred saw him coming, he sprang up and darted forward, sword and shield at the ready, but he could not deflect the weapon, which Arthur thrust at him with such great force that it went straight through his breastplate and into his heart. With one last scream of hatred, anger and pain, Mordred dragged himself forward on the spear, raised his sword in both hands and brought it crashing down on Arthur's head. Then he staggered backward and fell to the ground with a final, terrible groan.

Arthur sank slowly to his knees. Bedivere and Lucan were there to catch him as he fell, blood gushing from a deep wound where the sword had pierced his helmet.

"Take me to Lake Avalon," he whispered.

With great difficulty, the two wounded knights carried Arthur to the lake and laid him on the grass under an oak tree. Gentle waves lapped the shore in the moonlight. A fine mist covered the water, just as it had when Arthur had first set eyes on the lake, so many years before.

The exertion had been too much for Lucan. His final task over, he lay down next to Arthur, shut his eyes and died. Bedivere sobbed quietly at his side.

"There's no time for tears," said Arthur softly. "I have one more task for you to do. . . the last I may ever ask of you. Take Excalibur, go to the water, throw it in. . . then tell me what happens. My sight has gone now. Darkness is all I see."

Bedivere took hold of Excalibur and went down to the lake. He heaved the sword high into the air, flinging it as far as he could across the lake. Just as it was about to plunge into the water, a small white hand shot up through the mist and caught it by the handle. The silver blade glistened in the moonlight momentarily before it was drawn slowly down, back beneath the deep, dark waters.

Bedivere staggered back to Arthur and told him what he had seen.

"Then all is well," whispered the king. "And what do you see now?"

"Nothing but mist and moonlight, Sir."

"Then look again," croaked Arthur, unable to lift his head. Bedivere peered through the darkness, scanning the mist-covered lake. A gleaming barge was gliding across the water, with a tall figure in flowing white robes standing at the prow. It was the Lady of the Lake, magically risen from the dead to take Arthur to his resting place.

"Help me to the boat,"

whispered Arthur.

Bedivere half dragged, half carried Arthur down to the barge. The lady helped the king on board and laid him down, cradling his wounded head tenderly in her lap.

"Do not leave me, my king," Bedivere pleaded. "What is to become of Logres once you are gone?"

"I must go to the Isle of Avalon," called Arthur. The barge was drifting slowly out into the lake. "But I will return one day when my kingdom needs me." These were the dying king's final words. Bedivere sat down on the shore as the barge floated slowly away and disappeared into the night.

Lancelot reached Logres the next day. When he asked for news of Arthur, he was told that the king had marched westward. Then he was shown Gawain's grave near the beach. There he spent several hours in prayer and contemplation, before leaving his men and galloping toward Avalon.

At nightfall, he stopped for shelter in an old abbey in the forest. As he was led through the cloisters, he passed a group of nuns. One of them uttered a cry and fell to the ground. Lancelot kneeled to help her. The tearful face that stared up at him was strangely familiar.

Gone were the long, flowing tresses, the embroidered robes and the sweet, innocent smile, but her eyes were as bright as on the day they had first met. It was Guinevere.

She told him about everything that had happened: Mordred's treachery, her escape to the tower and of Arthur's last battle, which she had heard about in a message from Bedivere. Then, with a wail of sorrow, she declared that all the death and destruction had been brought about by their love, and that now they must live lives of repentance and vow never to see each other again. Lancelot would have done anything for Guinevere, but this was almost too much to bear. He said a last, tearful goodbye and rode off into the forest with a broken heart. There was nothing left to fight for, and he had no friends left on earth.

One night, many years later, he dreamed that Guinevere was dying. He rode straight to the abbey the next morning, to discover that she had passed away peacefully in the night. From that moment Lancelot lost all will to live and refused to eat or drink. Within a fortnight he too was dead. Of the other Knights of the Round Table, only Bedivere survived. He spent the rest of his days living as a hermit, deep in the forest.

So what became of King Arthur? To this day, no one really knows. Some say he died of his wound and was buried on the Isle of Avalon, where a simple gravestone bears the inscription:

HERE LIES ARTHUR,
THE ONCE AND FUTURE KING

Others say that he was healed by the Lady of the Lake and now he and Merlin, together with the Knights of the Round Table, are sleeping, deep in a mountain cave somewhere in Wales. One day, they say, when the kingdom is in terrible danger, they will awake from centuries of slumber, and the clanking of armor will be heard once more as King Arthur and the Knights of the Round Table go galloping through the land.

WHO'S WHO IN THE STORIES

SIR ACCOLON OF GAUL

Family: Not known. **Career:** Lover of Morgan le Fay. Used by her in a plot to kill King Arthur; but Arthur, disguised as Sir Ontzlake, killed Accolon. **Personality:** Ambitious and brave, but gullible. **Status:** Knight of Gaul. **Attributes:** Physically strong. Good fighter.

SIR AGRAVAIN

Family: Younger brother of Gawain. **Career:** Joined with Mordred to plot against Arthur. Killed by Sir Lancelot. **Personality:** Resentful, sly and suspicious. **Status:** Knight of the Round Table. **Attributes:** Not a very good knight.

KING ANGWISH

Family: Father of Iseult and husband of Queen Isaud. **Career:** As King of Ireland, made peace with Cornwall by sending his daughter Iseult to marry King Mark. Saved Tristram from execution. **Personality:** Kind, thoughtful. **Status:** King of Ireland. **Attributes:** Generous and wise.

KING ARTHUR

Family: Son of King Uther Pendragon and Duchess Igrayne. Husband of Guinevere. Brother of Anna. Half-brother of Morgan le Fay. **Career:** Brought up by Sir Ector. Removed a sword from a stone to become king. Given the sword Excalibur by the Lady of the Lake. Ruled Logres for many years. Tricked by Morgan le Fay and betrayed by Mordred, who killed him in the last battle. **Personality:** Kind, tolerant, brave, polite. **Status:** King of Logres. **Attributes:** Excellent fighter and leader.

SIR BALAN

Family: Younger brother of Sir Balyn. **Career:** Defeated the Knight of the Island and was forced to take his place. Accidentally killed his brother Balyn, and was killed by him, as a result of the curse of Balyn's sword. **Personality:** Friendly and kind. **Status:** Knight of the Round Table. **Attributes:** Small, but a strong fighter.

SIR BALYN

Family: Brother of Sir Balan. **Career:** Cursed by an evil, enchanted sword he won from a visiting damsel, he wounded King Pelles. He and his brother Sir Balan killed each other in single combat while in disguise. **Personality:** Shy and quiet, until he won the cursed sword and became aggressive and arrogant. **Status:** Knight of the Round Table. **Attributes:** Pure-hearted.

SIR BERCILAK/THE GREEN KNIGHT

Family: Not known. **Career:** Was changed into the Green Knight by Morgan le Fay to test the bravery of the Knights of the Round Table. **Personality:** Generous, jovial. As the Green Knight, fierce, brave and frightening. **Status:** Lord. **Attributes:** As the Green Knight, able to replace his head after it was cut off.

SIR BORS

Family: Son of King Bors of Gaul, and nephew of Sir Lancelot. **Career:** Spent many years searching for Lancelot, and defected to Lancelot's side when he and Arthur were at war. **Personality:** Dedicated and honest. **Status:** Knight of the Round Table. **Attributes:** Big and strong, a good fighter.

LADY BRUSEN

Family: Not known. **Career:** Learned witchcraft from Morgan le Fay, and used it to help Princess Elaine trick Lancelot. **Personality:** Cunning, deceitful. **Status:** Lady-in-waiting. **Attributes:** Able to work magic.

SIR ECTOR

Family: Foster-father of King Arthur, father of Sir Kay. **Career:** Brought up Arthur from birth on Merlin's orders. **Personality:** Patient, kind. **Status:** Knight. **Attributes:** Trustworthy. Loyal.

PRINCESS ELAINE

Family: Daughter of King Pelles, wife of Lancelot and mother of Lancelot's son, Galahad. **Career:** Tricked Lancelot into marrying her by disguising herself as Guinevere, with the help of Lady Brusen. **Personality:** Selfish, silly. **Status:** Princess. **Attributes:** Very pretty.

SIR GAHERIS

Family: Younger brother of Sir Gawain, nephew of Arthur, son of Queen Anna and King Lot of Orkney. **Career:** Came to Camelot as Gawain's squire. Killed by Lancelot during rescue of Guinevere. **Personality:** Courageous. **Status:** Knight of the Round Table. **Attributes:** Good fighter.

SIR GARETH/SIR LOVELYHANDS

Family: Younger brother of Gawain, nephew of Arthur. **Career:** Assigned to kitchen duties and nicknamed "Lovelyhands" by Sir Kay when he first came to Camelot, until he went on a quest and revealed his true identity. Killed by Lancelot during rescue of Guinevere. **Personality:** Humble, but brave. **Status:** Knight of the Round Table. **Attributes:** Good fighter. Clever.

SIR GARLON

Family: Not known. **Career:** Attacked strangers and spread fear and destruction, until he was killed by Sir Balyn at King Pelles's feast. **Personality:** Cruel and evil. **Status:** Knight. **Attributes:** Able to make himself invisible.

SIR GAWAIN

Family: Eldest son of King Lot and Queen Anna. Arthur's nephew. **Career:** Undertook quest for the Green Chapel to prove his worth. Fought and quested bravely on many occasions; helped Arthur on the quest set by Sir Gromer Somer Joure. Married Lady Ragnell. Avenged his brothers' deaths by inciting Arthur to fight Lancelot. Fatally wounded by Lancelot in the siege of Benwick. Wrote a letter of reconciliation to Lancelot on his deathbed. **Personality:** Brave, courteous and honorable, implacable when angry. **Status:** Knight of the Round Table. **Attributes:** Excellent knight. Good adviser.

GOUVERNALE

Family: Not known. **Career:** Helped to bring up Tristram and went with him to Cornwall, then to Ireland, where they both worked as court musicians. Saved Tristram from being killed by Queen Isaud. **Personality:** Kind, caring. **Status:** Servant and guardian. **Attributes:** Kind, loyal and reliable.

THE GREEN KNIGHT
see SIR BERCILAK

QUEEN GUINEVERE

Family: Daughter of King Leodegrance and wife of King Arthur. **Career:** Tried to be loyal to Arthur but was affected by her undying love for her champion Sir Lancelot, and also flirted with other knights. Lancelot rescued her when she was kidnapped by Sir Melligrance and when she was sentenced to death by Arthur. Became a nun after Arthur's last battle. **Personality:** Charming and clever, but sometimes moody and selfish. **Status:** Queen of Logres. **Attributes:** Great beauty.

SIR HECTOR

Family: Brother of Sir Lancelot. **Career:** Left Camelot for a long time and only returned after meeting Sir Percival and Sir Lancelot on his travels. **Personality:** Down-to-earth, caring. **Status:** Knight of the Round Table. **Attributes:** Quiet, wise, a good fighter.

LADY HEURODIS

Family: Wife of Sir Orfeo. **Career:** Bitten by a snake and abducted by the King of the Underworld. Returned ten years later after Sir Orfeo rescued her. **Personality:** Kind, witty and loving. **Status:** Ruler of Kent. **Attributes:** Beautiful. Good singer.

QUEEN ISAUD

Family: Wife of King Angwish, mother of Iseult, and sister of Sir Marhault. **Career:** Healed Tristram's wound, but later attacked him when she discovered his identity. Made love-potion for Iseult and King Mark, which Tristram and Iseult accidentally drank. **Personality:** Unpredictable. **Status:** Queen of Ireland. Sorceress. **Attributes:** Able to cast spells and heal wounds.

PRINCESS ISEULT

Family: Daughter of King Angwish and Queen Isaud of Ireland. **Career:** Fell in love with Tristram, but was forced to marry King Mark of Cornwall. **Personality:** Realistic, but romantic. **Status:** Princess of Ireland, Queen of Cornwall. **Attributes:** Very beautiful.

SIR KAY

Family: Son of Sir Ector and foster-brother of King Arthur. **Career:** Brought up alongside Arthur. Came to Camelot when Arthur became king. Killed in the last battle. **Personality:** Rude, scornful and boastful. **Status:** Knight of the Round Table. **Attributes:** Not a very good knight.

THE LADY OF THE LAKE

Family: Not known. **Career:** Gave Arthur the sword Excalibur, and appeared several times to warn and advise him. Raised Lancelot and brought him to the Round Table to become a knight. Was killed by Balyn under the influence of the cursed sword, but returned magically at the end of Arthur's life to lead him to the Isle of Avalon. **Personality:** Mysterious, enigmatic. **Status:** A lake fairy. **Attributes:** Beauty. Magical powers.

SIR LANCELOT DU LAKE

Family: Son of King Ban and Queen Elaine. Husband of Princess Elaine. **Career:** Left near a lake by his mother, and raised by the Lady of the Lake, who later brought him to Camelot on Merlin's orders. Became Guinevere's champion and fell in love with her. Was tricked into marrying Elaine and went insane, but later returned to

Camelot. Killed forty knights, including Sir Gaheris and Sir Gareth, in the process of rescuing Guinevere from being burned at the stake. Exiled to France by Arthur. Challenged to fight by Sir Gawain, whom he wounded fatally. On his return to Logres he found that Arthur was dead and that Guinevere had become a nun. Died of a broken heart shortly after Guinevere died. **Personality:** Brave, noble, fearless and romantic. **Status:** Knight of the Round Table, and Arthur's favorite knight. Champion of Queen Guinevere. **Attributes:** Excellent fighter. Handsome. Honorable.

SIR LAUNFAL

Family: Not known. **Career:** Fled Camelot after upsetting Guinevere, and became rich and successful after meeting a magical lady, Lady Tryamour, in the forest. **Personality:** Shy and self-effacing. **Status:** Knight of the Round Table. **Attributes:** Generous.

SIR LOVELYHANDS
see SIR GARETH

SIR MARHAULT

Family: Brother of Queen Isaud. **Career:** Fought Tristram, who gave him a fatal wound. **Personality:** Savage, aggressive. **Status:** Irish champion knight. **Attributes:** Immensely strong.

KING MARK

Family: Uncle of Tristram, husband of Iseult. **Career:** Ruled Cornwall. Sent Tristram to fetch Iseult from Ireland to be his wife. Banished Tristram when he discovered his love for Iseult. **Personality:** Selfish, weak-minded. **Status:** King of Cornwall. **Attributes:** A poor ruler.

SIR MELLIGRANCE

Family: Son of King Bagdemus. **Career:** Kidnapped Guinevere, who was rescued by Lancelot. **Personality:** Crafty and cowardly. **Status:** Knight of the Round Table. **Attributes:** Weak but cunning.

MERLETT

Family: Not known. **Career:** Served Sir Orfeo as his deputy, and took over the kingdom of Kent for the ten years Orfeo was away. **Personality:** Kind, caring, cheerful. **Status:** Deputy leader of Kent. **Attributes:** Very loyal.

MERLIN

Family: Son of Madog Morfryn and Aldan. **Career:** Adviser to Uther Pendragon, and then to Arthur. Took the baby Arthur from Tintagel Castle to Sir Ector, who brought him up. **Personality:** Mysterious, wise. **Status:** Sorcerer. **Attributes:** Able to cast spells, change shape and predict the future.

SIR MORDRED

Family: Possibly a nephew of King Arthur. **Career:** Plotted with Morgan le Fay to bring about Arthur's downfall. Usurped the throne and tried to marry Guinevere while Arthur was in France. Was killed by Arthur in the last battle. His final blow killed Arthur. **Personality:** Devious, malicious. **Status:** Knight of the Round Table. **Attributes:** Good fighter.

MORGAN LE FAY

Family: Daughter of Gorlois and Igrayne, Duke and Duchess of Cornwall. Half-sister of Arthur, wife of Sir Uriens of Gore, mother of Uwain. **Career:** Learned magic from Merlin. Plotted against the Round Table. Sent Mordred to Camelot to stir up trouble. **Personality:** Scheming, evil. **Status:** Sorceress. **Attributes:** Able to cast spells and change shape. Not as powerful as Merlin.

SIR ORFEO

Family: Not known. **Career:** Ruled Kent until his wife Heurodis was stolen away by a mysterious king. Went to live in the wilderness and lived in poverty for ten years. Eventually found Heurodis, won her back by playing his harp, and returned to Kent. **Personality:** Kind, hospitable, emotional. **Status:** Ruler of Kent. **Attributes:** Skilled musician.

KING PELLES

Family: Son of King Pellam. Father of Elaine. **Career:** Crippled by Sir Balyn, he wanted to keep Lancelot at Carbonek as his son-in-law, by way of retribution. **Personality:** Proud, selfish. **Status:** King of Castle Carbonek. **Attributes:** Cunning.

SIR PELLINORE

Family: Father of Sir Tor, Sir Lamerok, Sir Percival, Sir Agglovale and Sir Dornar, all Knights of the Round Table. **Career:** Fought Arthur before he became his ally. Killed by Gawain in revenge for killing his father King Lot of Orkney. **Personality:** Fierce, aggressive, belligerent. **Status:** Knight of the Round Table. **Attributes:** Fearless fighter.

SIR PERCIVAL

Family: Son of Pellinore. **Career:** Brought up in the forest in Wales until the age of sixteen, when he met some Knights of the Round Table and decided to leave for Camelot and become a knight. Went to Camelot and retrieved Arthur's golden goblet when it was stolen. **Personality:** Keen, brave, though sometimes too hasty. **Status:** Knight of the Round Table. **Attributes:** A very good knight.

SIR TRISTRAM

Family: Son of King Meliodas and Queen Elizabeth of Lyonesse; nephew of King Mark. **Career:** Became a champion knight of Cornwall, and defeated Sir Marhault, who wounded him. Went to Ireland to find a cure for his wound, and fell in love with Princess Iseult. Caught kissing her after she was married to Mark, and was banished from Cornwall before joining the Round Table. **Personality:** Charming and clever. **Status:** Prince of Lyonesse, Knight of the Round Table. **Attributes:** Excellent fighter and chivalrous knight.

SIR URIENS OF GORE

Family: Husband of Morgan le Fay. Father of Uwain. **Career:** Tricked by Morgan le Fay's damsels on enchanted ship. Morgan le Fay then tried to kill him, but was thwarted by Uwain. **Personality:** Too trusting. Not very bright. **Status:** Knight of the Round Table. **Attributes:** Not a good knight.

WHO WAS ARTHUR?

King Arthur is a legendary king of Britain who has appeared in stories and folk tales ever since medieval times (about 1000-1500 AD). He is supposed to have lived in the Dark Ages, which is a name for the time after the Romans left Britain ~ about 400-700AD. He is said to have been a heroic leader who fought off invaders and successfully conquered many lands.

DID ARTHUR REALLY EXIST?

Although many of the stories about King Arthur have been made up by writers and storytellers, they may still be based on a real historical person. Some medieval historians wrote about a general or chieftain called Arthur, who died in a battle in about 540AD, along with "Medraut" ~ who may be the person behind the character of Mordred.

WHERE THE STORIES CAME FROM

Legendary tales of Arthur and his knights first began to appear in the 12th century, when a British historian, Geoffrey of Monmouth, wrote about Arthur in a book called *The History of the Kings of Britain*. However, although this was called a history book, it was probably, in fact, mostly made up!

Geoffrey's version includes Merlin the magician, Guinevere, Mordred and "Walwain" ~ another name for Gawain.

Later, the stories were developed into much longer versions by other writers, including a French writer called Chrétien de Troyes, and the legends began to spread throughout Europe. Then, in the 15th century,

an English knight, Sir Thomas Malory, translated the tales from French back into English, in a very long book called *Le Morte D'Arthur* (The Death of Arthur). Malory is thought to have written *Le Morte D'Arthur* while he was serving a long prison sentence. Despite its title, it tells the story of Arthur's whole life, as well as many of the adventures of the Knights of the Round Table.

Most of the tales in this book are based on Malory's stories. Some, though, such as "Gawain and Lady Ragnell" and "Sir Launfal", are based on long individual poems known as Romances. These were popular in Europe in medieval times. They are usually anonymous, and tell the stories of knights and their adventures.

MORE ABOUT ARTHUR

Many writers through the ages have retold the legends of King Arthur. For example, in the 19th century, the poet Alfred Tennyson wrote about Arthur in his poem *The Idylls of the King*. *The Sword in the Stone*, by T. H. White, is a novel about Arthur's childhood. Stories of King Arthur's life have also been made into many films and cartoons.

Although no one really knows whether the Round Table existed, or where Camelot was, there are still some parts of Britain that are connected with Arthur. Some people say he is buried at Glastonbury Tor, in Somerset, England. You can also visit Tintagel, in Cornwall, where he is supposed to have been born. Many of the other places mentioned in this book, such as Carlisle, the Wirral, Orkney and Kent, are still real parts of Britain.